STATIC FLUX

Static Flux
© 2018 Natasha Young
ISBN 978-1-988355-13-9

Published by Metatron Press
305-6545 Ave. Durocher
Montreal, Quebec
H3N 1Z7

www.metatron.press

First printing

Cover design | Anjela Freyja
Author photo | Christopher Honeywell
Editor | Ashley Obscura

STATIC FLUX

NATASHA YOUNG

"A woman is always accompanied, except when quite alone—and perhaps even then—by her own image of herself."

– John Berger

It was the first cold day of autumn, coming off a humid summer in the psychic confines of northern Brooklyn. I was at a cocktail bar at dinnertime on a Wednesday. The room was candlelit and otherwise empty, darker still than the gloaming that descended outside as the streetlights flickered on. I had come to drink undisturbed.

"On the house, doll," the bartender said without irony, as she placed a French 75 on the bar for me. I was so cash poor it was the least and most I could do to raise the coupe in my hand, my wrist rigid with fear of spilling a drop.

"To childhood's end," I toasted her. "The day you realize you'll never become the person you dreamed you'd be."

On any given night I had a friend tending bar at one of the neighborhood haunts. We shared the sense of having been deprived, by circumstance or late capitalism, our destined Artist's Life: unstructured free time, solitude, space, all much too expensive in this city. For keeping them company during their shift, I drank for free and padded their pockets in what tips I could manage at the end of the night.

Tonight, Misha was behind the bar. She was slight, mild-mannered, extensively tattooed, with hair dyed jet-black and cut with laser precision in a flapper's bob, shaved clean at the nape. She stood only a head higher than the bar in her platforms. She carried herself with grace, maintained ballerina posture even after hours on her feet in her Docs. In soft contradiction to her tough-as-nails aesthetic, her body language betrayed the prideful, egoic upkeep of her unrealized dream of being a dancer; her hardness, a reckoning with the interminable student loan repayments she owed for an abortive stint at NYU.

A portly Hasidic man entered and sauntered up to the bar. I sensed right away his sense of entitlement to my company, his passive-aggressive friendliness. I willed myself to be smaller, to take up no more space than the diameter of the stool. The man sat down on the stool beside me, despite the rest of the bar being empty.

Misha greeted him like they were familiar: "Hey, Sol." She placed a glass of water in front of him. He turned to me and grasped my hand, awkwardly by the knuckles of my fingers, said "Hello, hello, so nice to meet you."

I grimaced as close as I could to a smile and withdrew my hands. He excused himself to the restroom and I whispered to Misha across the bar, "Is he the landlord or something?" "No, he just comes in once in awhile," she said, with a posed look.

When he returned and took his seat beside me, he declined Misha's offer of wine but sipped the water. I was perched still on the stool, anxious and alert, my gaze focused on the rim of my drink as I avoided eye contact while he made an insistent effort to get me to talk.

Sol was a happy aberration. He explained to me, sounding guileless, that he liked to gather forbidden intel on the world outside his Orthodox community. He was curious like a child about a woman like me, he said. Women like me didn't exist in his world. I was amused, but suspicious. I took my hands off the bar and thought about getting up to leave, but Misha had already made me another drink and set it down before me. Sol leaned in closer, then, to confide in me, his voice lowered—unnecessarily, though, as no one else was around.

"Sometimes I try on my wife's clothes."

"I think that's great," I said. "To be honest, I wish more men would try it."

He chortled.

"I like you, young lady!"

"Does *she* know about it?"

"My wife?!" He imitated her to demonstrate her horrified reaction, a rather cruel caricature. He spoke in a high-pitched squeal and contorted his face to look mean. I thought I'd be twisted, too, if I was a woman living under his orthodoxy.

"She even refuses to wear pants. I've begged her to try on a pair—it's usually forbidden for our women, but I say, 'Dear, just try on my trousers, just once, to see how it feels! Women wear pants all the time!' But even in private, she refuses. I believe in equality for women, by the way—which, believe me, very few of us do."

I shot back the rest of my drink and motioned to Misha for a refill.

"Nobody knows I come out like this. At least, I hope not. No, they can't. Because if they did, they'd have cast me out by now."

"They do that?"

"Oh, yes. They're very easily scandalized. I'd be exiled."

"That's rough."

A pause in the talking brought me a moment of relief.

"What do you do in life, my dear?"

"Nothing."

"You're mysterious! That's alright. I'm not bothered leaving some things unknown."

"What?"

"More fun that way." He winked.

He took a napkin and Misha's pen from the bar and wrote on it, in childlike script, his email address. I was surprised he had one. It was a secret from his family. He checked it only in the public library, he said, and then announced that he had to go home. I nodded and waved goodbye as he waddled out the door, turning south. Misha minded her work behind the bar.

"Everybody's just looking for a way out," I said.

"Did you hear about the school shooting?" she said.

"Another one?!"

"This morning."

"No. I've been avoiding the news. Jesus fucking Christ."

"I know."

"I feel numb. Not, like, indifferent. I mean, like, depressed to the point of numbness."

"Everybody feels that today. Everybody but Sol, apparently."

"Oblivion must be a pleasant place to live."

She lifted her eyes from her busy hands with a look I felt was made to humor me, and shrugged. Our conversations often trailed off this way. Her pitch-black bob hung like a satin curtain along her jawbone.

I hung around until she closed up, then we stepped outside, lit our cigarettes, and bounced on our heels to keep warm. In my sighs of resignation were 7,000 chemicals, including hundreds of toxins and about 70 known carcinogens.

Walking north along the East River towards home, I shivered as much from anxiety as from the chill in the air. I was imagining how I might defend myself if attacked along the row of industrial warehouses. No signs of life around, as far as I could tell, but the city was comprised of hiding places.

I started—something rustled in a pile of garbage bags on the sidewalk in front of me. A rat crossed my path. I walked on, unsteady, but with a sense of urgency. I cut around a building on the river, winding through construction barriers for the new condos rising up out of the craggy shoreline across the water from Midtown. I'd passed the ferry dock and started up the stairs, through the newly renovated park, when I saw a shadow in motion, in the faint cast of a street light stretched across the clean concrete. I proceeded with slower, softer steps, toward the dim spotlight. Looked like a small, gangly wolf—I remembered reading somewhere that the coywolf, a crossbreed born of desperation and resource scarcity, had proliferated in the city. The coywolf stopped his strolling in his tracks as we met eyes. Still for a moment. I took a slow step forward. He looked at me, surprised, and bounded off, disappeared through a hole in the orange plastic netting round the concrete barriers, into the dark construction site.

Still drunk, I climbed six flights of stairs to the apartment I shared with my boyfriend, Marcel. He was away on holiday with his family—a "real" African safari, for which he'd left a week ago. His mother had planned the trip as a surprise. I made a fight out of it because the trip would overlap with my birthday, and of course I had not been invited. In the days leading up to his departure, I made my resentment for his going without me obvious: withdrawn from conversation, barbed reactions to his affection.

I opened a window and climbed out onto the fire escape to smoke a cigarette. He didn't know I smoked, or so I thought. As much as I could help it, I showed him my best self. I would only smoke when I was drinking with friends without him, or when I was upset with him, but that was remarkably rare. In the mire of naïveté that was my early twenties, I wasn't yet self-aware enough to comprehend my dishonesty as a form of disloyalty. I wondered what time it was wherever he was. Every muscle in my body tensed up in the damp wind as I struggled to light one.

I wanted to sleep, but dreaded going to bed alone. I reflected how pathetic it was that, if one of the little jalopy planes he'd be on in Africa were to crash, or if he'd be blown up by terrorists, or his family hijacked for ransom money, the last words exchanged between us would have been an argument.

"Can't you be happy for me? I'd be happy for you if you were going away to do something you really wanted, even though I would miss you."

"It's never me who leaves, though. I never get to do anything fun."

I honestly believed I did not deserve him. It was the only thing we fought over. With surgical precision he excised and analyzed my self-sabotaging behavioral patterns. He said there were much bigger things in store for me; that I was destined for greatness, if only I could get out of my own way. If only I could internalize his belief in me. But all I could think of was all that I lacked, the experiences I hadn't had, people I hadn't met, places I hadn't been. Having grown up poor, among rural New England folk of no pedigree, what I wanted seemed impossible. And what I wanted most of all was to be a writer, and not poor.

I climbed back inside from the fire escape, filled a glass with ice and poured myself some of his good whisky (I hated whisky), and sat down at my laptop to get some work done. Work typically meant writing content for brands to supplement my "real" life's work—cultural criticism and journalism—for which the pay was meager and never on time. I couldn't afford the career I'd had my heart set on pursuing. Even entry-level editorial assistant jobs seemed to exist solely for designer-educated progeny whose lifestyles were supplemented by a legacy of wealth extending at least as far back as the baby boom. They didn't pay more than twenty-five to thirty thousand a year, at a time when average rent for a closet-sized, windowless room in Bushwick already exceeded one thousand dollars a month.

Sharing an apartment with Marcel offset the cost of living just enough for me to make it. We split the rent, but sometimes he paid more than his share to help me out. He swore he didn't mind so long as I was doing my best and not taking advantage of him. I maintained hope in an old-fashioned work ethic, took on excruciatingly boring freelance copywriting gigs and temp jobs. I had no insurance; I hoped nothing would happen that would require my hospitalization, in which event I hoped for a quick death. I was sitting at the kitchen table we'd found on the street a few months ago and carried home together for about ten blocks. I was staring into the bleak light of a blank document. I sipped the whisky and screwed up my face in disgust. I had been living with Marcel in that modest apartment for six months. I'd moved in only a month into dating him.

I met Marcel on a Greyhound bus. I was on the way to visit my parents. The reason for the visit was to let them feed me while I had a mental breakdown.

At the time I was an unpaid editorial intern at *Art Journal*, a career opportunity I could not afford to take, and which I had been working several part-time jobs to support. I just couldn't hold any one of them down for long. At one point I was a barback and cashier at a third-wave coffee joint in Williamsburg. When I wasn't too clumsy, I was too slow. I was forbidden from operating the espresso machine. I shoveled snow outside the café at 5 a.m., my face always beet red from whipping winds by the time we'd open. Exhausted, after the first hour of dealing with customers, I'd tidy up, wash dishes— anything to avoid further interaction. I was fired after about three weeks.

Then I worked at a boutique that catered to fashion's pretentious new wave. I sold thousand-dollar miniature camera bags to women my age, who were a lot like me in a generational/cultural sense, but virtually poreless and without the fear of homelessness in their hearts. I sold six-hundred-dollar Japanese cotton T-shirts designed to look sixteen sizes too big to white guys with store-bought personalities. I had to wrap things in tissue paper with excruciating care: "a mindful practice, like ikebana," the manager said.

I took orders over the phone occasionally from clients, or their personal shoppers. This went on for a week before it occurred to me to copy down the credit card information for personal use. It was a boon for about a month until the day the manager brought me into the back of the store for a chat with the company's lawyer. They had me sign something my eyes were too hot with shame-tears to read, then gave me my last pay and set me free.

During this period I wrote nothing.

By far the easiest way I'd found to supplement my income was to masturbate theatrically on live webcam for strange men who'd pay by the minute to masturbate to me. My screenname was CallaFornication. It started in a moment of desperation, but as soon as I got over the initial dejection I found it to be an elegant solution to whatever was wrong with me. I regarded myself in the mirror image of a digital windowpane, fussed with my hair, adjusted the awkward positioning of my body in relation to the laptop to optimize the angle, position, pose. I wasn't obligated to see any nude image but my own on my screen, but certain strange men would pay in the hundreds for one-on-one time, usually silent, just wanting someone to watch them back. The quiet ones were the only pleasure, aside from money. It was a pleasant surprise to encounter shy sweetness, there of all places, in the liminal space into which the camera's lens vacuums the ego. Mostly it was commands barked anonymously into the chat box, like "look me in the eyes when u cum," and I would obediently look into the eye of the camera while I faked an orgasm the likes of which I'd never actually experienced.

I had blocked viewing access to all IP addresses in New York state, but often wondered who among these strange men was physically closest to me. As soon as the thrifty ones came they'd disconnect. Still I held out hope that I served some noble purpose to these men, somehow, who had lives, responsibilities, loved ones, things to do and people to see. Perhaps one of my patrons was a noble male feminist, donating to the cause of broke girls who didn't want to be touched; another, a reformed hedonist, trying his best to remain technically faithful to his spouse.

But that, too, was an unsustainable performance, and it became too depressing to feign getting off. And then after my rent check had been late three months in a row, my roommates held a surprise "house meeting" and said I had to move out at the end of the month. So I got on the next bus out of town.

First I saw him in the window seat, then saw that my designated seat was right beside him. He was fair with dark hair long enough to brush his shoulders, silver Henry Miller-esque glasses perched on his aquiline nose, and, behind them, kind, grey-blue eyes. His face was a few days unshaven. He was focused on the laptop in front of him, with headphones on, but glanced up and smiled at me. I put my headphones on and dialed in a ten-plus-minute ambient track by Brian Eno, felt a slight release of my vice-grip tension. He watched solemnly out the window as we left the city. I watched him watching us go. We had just passed the Guggenheim when I noticed his body relaxing into sleep. I took the opportunity to study closer his sweet sleeping face, his hair tucked behind his ear, his hands relaxed on his lap. Suddenly his body jolted—the muscles in his legs jumped as he was relaxing into sleep. The abrupt release of force startled me, and startled him awake, too. We made eye contact. He blushed hard. We both laughed.

"I'm so sorry," he said, "I don't usually do that."

"I wonder what that is. When you're falling asleep and your body flinches like that," I said.

"In German we call it *einschlafzuckungen*."

I laughed and immediately worried I was being rude.

"I'm sorry, it's just, it seems like there's a German word for any obscure phenomenon one could possibly think of."

"Oh no, don't worry. It is funny."

"You're German?"

"Swiss. But I'm from the German part, Zürich."

"Ah," I said and looked at my hands in my lap.

"I'm Marcel. What is your name?"

Marcel explained he was on the way to a conference on oncology, immunology, and microbiology in Cambridge. He'd gotten his Ph.D. at the university back in Zürich. "They start you younger there, so Ph.D.s don't take so long," he said.

The incline of his neck suggested poor posture, surely from the ten thousand hours spent slouching over laboratory tables. Our conversation flowed into an immediate intimacy, the kind that frightens and excites both parties, and I observed his mannerisms to the detail with an overwhelming sense of tenderness. He'd shift expressions, instantly self-conscious, when he'd made a bad joke or said something too sincere. His eyes would dart back and forth over my face, looking for a reaction. Watching his mannerisms, I could see the wheels turning in his head as if with my third eye: each time his countenance shifted, it was in tandem with his internal shifts, expressed in finely choreographed arrangements he'd been developing all his life. It was all his, this unique beauty, this nervous grammar to his body language. To my surprise, he said he felt as if we'd already known each other for a long time, and I agreed.

I asked him what, in his opinion so far, was the biggest difference between America and Europe.

"God, there are so many."

"Don't worry, I won't take it personally."

"I think Americans are held back by issues we do not have as much trouble with anymore," he said, slowly and with care. "Problems with civility and human dignity. Realpolitik, money and class as political problems. In Switzerland, our taxes are high, but our people are paid well. We are taken care of. It means something that we pay high taxes. I think our teachers make around seven thousand."

"Seven thousand Euros?! That's insane."

"You think they shouldn't be paid that much?"

"What? Wait, do you you mean seven thousand per *month*?"

"Yes, month."

"Oh. Here we think in terms of, like, annually."

He looked surprised.

"If we were to say our salary for the year, the number

is too big. We could not understand it in terms of day-to-day life. It is easier to relate to the monthly expenses, I think, not to be overwhelmed. But yes, our teachers, they earn much more than teachers here."

"That's how it should be," I said.

"Of course, we have problems, too—but we've already been through the adolescence of our society, so perhaps we are more advanced in learning how to solve these problems. We have a rather long historical framework to reference."

"This country is just irresponsible to its own detriment. We let each other suffer unnecessarily and it holds us all back," I said. "It's such bullshit. The government is supposedly of the people, but if that's the case, then we are a lazy and apathetic populace. The powerful don't leave enough to go around for the rest of us. They lack empathy. Their self-serving policy changes perpetuate ignorance and poverty."

"Health care crises, debt crises, fighting with the other countries," he said, "these are juvenile problems. Whereas my country takes care of its own, so our problems go deeper, so deep they're complex problems of the collective mind—problems of perception of value.

We are concerned with ethics and new morality without religion, how to make society even more equitable, how to quell extremism. Our problems are how to defeat the outdated opinions that exist still in the minds of people. We can see that for the future we must turn to language, to debate our ideas about justice. Or else we have no future. Americans are not there with us yet."

"Between the pitiful lack of access to mental health care in this country, our affinity for reckless violence, and our systematic failure to accept responsibility for and to learn from our mistakes," I complained, "I don't feel optimistic about the future."

"Oh, certainly it's not that bad."

"You don't have to be concerned for my nonexistent national pride."

"It is not even a point of pride, you see, but pragmatism. I don't think Europe is all that better, per se, just that Europe is an older, more mature society. America is a young country. Like a teenager, America thinks it knows everything—is that the right pronoun? He? She? It?—"

"Don't get me started on gender pronouns," I said, but he didn't seem to get it.

"What I mean to say is that America has the arrogance of youth," he continued. "We who watch from outside see transparently how deeply Americans are in denial of their actual status and relation to the rest of the world."

"Youth, arrogance, and denial go hand-in-hand-in-hand."

"They think they're justified in everything because they're the chosen ones. Such arrogance. Just like a child. The rest of us can only hope this country will grow up before a third world war happens."

"Considering this country was founded by the craziest outcast zealots during one of Europe's many violent colonial outbursts, I wouldn't hold my breath," I said, and he smiled like he'd just figured something out about me.

"You are a lot of fun to talk to," he said, and I blushed.

We talked nonstop the entire ride, went over our life stories. We disembarked together in Boston, sat on a park bench, and kept going. Time grew long and I had a connection to catch, so he gave me his phone number and said to be in touch.

Aweek later, I returned to New York on a desperate mission to find new shelter. I'd taken out a new line of credit to afford a security deposit, but the search was futile, and I had no income to prove in the daunting application process. Drunk at Misha's bar again one night, I texted him.

I was mortified when I woke near noon the next day, deathly hungover, and he'd responded early that morning. He wanted to see me that night for dinner. I drank coconut water, smoked a joint on the stoop, ate a bagel smeared inches-thick with cream cheese and topped with lox. I had nothing interesting to talk about and too much to hide. I did nothing, knew no one, had no money, no great stories to tell. I hated myself and wanted to die. I replied, "Yes I'll see you there."

I met him at a piano bar with an incomprehensible wine list. I assumed an aloof pose and, uninterested in trying, let him pick everything, let uncomfortable silences lapse in between reactions and responses, couldn't think of anything even halfway charming. I was surprised when he offered to walk me home.

"Did you have a nice evening?" he said.

"Yes, everything was lovely."

"I thought you may have been in a bad mood."

"Not particularly, this is just how I am sometimes."

"Is something wrong?"

"Probably. I don't know."

He was quiet for a minute.

"Are you depressed?"

"Did you just diagnose me?"

"Am I wrong?"

"That's not the point."

"I just want you to know it's not a burden you have to hide from me. You can talk to me."

"A mood disorder is not what I'd consider fodder for making a good impression on a date."

"Do you talk to anyone about it?"

"Clearly not. Therapy is expensive."

I saw the corners of his mouth slide downward and realized, to my surprise, that he was genuinely sympathetic to my situation.

"I didn't mean to make you feel bad. I'm sorry. I am in a shit mood."

"That's fine. You don't have to discount my concerns like that."

"I didn't know you cared."

He sighed and sounded annoyed.

"Of course I do." He hailed us a taxi and asked the driver to drop me home first.

We arrived at my apartment building off Bedford and Grand in Williamsburg, the one from which I was about to be evicted. It was a shoebox room in a legacy-lease loft on the second floor of a two-storey commercial-zoned brick block, right above an iconic bagel joint, which had just closed down after the landlord jacked up the rent 300%. The leaseholder, a classic New York JAP with a commensurate wit, had been living there since before gentrification struck, so she had a good deal, but she was fighting the landlord in city court to combat a similar rent increase being imposed on her. When I moved in, she warned me that we might all have to vacate the apartment suddenly one day if he won the case. But it was so gorgeous, with its old, hardwood floors and twelve-foot-high ceilings, that I couldn't walk away.

I snuck Marcel into the apartment, past my roommates, who obviously hated me and were watching a movie on the wall being screened by a projector, and into my bedroom. I removed his eyeglasses. He removed my clothes and undid his pants, shimmying them down his legs.

He lay back on my bed and guided me on top of him. It took some effort, some stretching, for him to fit himself entirely inside me. Holding my body close to his, he rocked me backwards so we both were sitting up, legs wrapped around one another, supporting the back of my head with one hand as he thrust his hips almost imperceptibly, penetrating slightly deeper with every micro movement. He maneuvered me onto my back, taking care not to hit my head on the foot of the clapboard bed frame while taking care, too, to remain inside of me. He put one of his hands on my throat while he steadied himself on the bed with the other, gently at first, until my knowing eye contact signaled him to take it further. It was the consensual element of surprise that pleased my body, though somewhere in my higher mind I troubled myself with why: why I enjoy threat in the vulnerable tenderness of intimacy. I willed my mind to shush, let the reptilian brain have its fun. We were not using a condom but, then again, the reptilian brain would have wanted for him to impregnate me. So I ignored those alarms, too, content to let my life burn down, leaving everything I had worked and fought for inside to suffocate and faint, with any luck, before burning to death.

We came at the same time, and my voice did something strange: the moan made glottal stops on its way out of my throat.

We slipped in and out of sleep, drenched in one another. Morning came too soon; I beheld the daylight with much hatred. We held each other while we talked and talked. He had so many questions, his countenance was so eager, his beaming eyes shone a hot strobe light right through me. Our faces were so close that to hide any thought or feeling seemed impossible.

I struggled to not feel self-conscious nude in the morning light while we carried on discussing trivialities like the simultaneous chaos and perfect order of the universe.

"Sometimes I think maybe all life is a physical manifestation of energy through which to channel more energy," he said with a yawn. "Perhaps the substance of consciousness is the most concentrated manifestation of energy."

"I like to think of the universe as a body whose neurons are stars," I said, "and we're all cells in that body, like we are the universe's consciousness, fragmented and dispersed in infinite directions to show the universe to itself from every perceivable angle. When a star dies, or when our brains die, the energy returns to the singular consciousness of the universe."

"Or the dream state is true reality, and the universe's formlessness functions as do we in the dream state: independent of the laws of physics and, simply put, organic life is the same as sending microscopic stereoscopic imaging apparatuses into the bloodstream. Even if the world is destroyed and all life upon it dies, it will be that the meta-consciousness has seen it all and it will collect itself to be redistributed elsewhere," he said.

My eyelids felt so heavy I may have already been dreaming when I posited aloud, for him to consider, that the electric currents in the burning center of our physical bodies fizzle out and depart but the same amount of elements remains fixed throughout the universe.

"Why do you think stars and the brain die? Because there is a limit to how much the universe's consciousness can be divided?"

"Perhaps," he said, "when the brain dies, a tiny black hole splits open where consciousness once was."

"Perhaps it really is, as David Lynch says, that some brains have more consciousness than others."

"Consciousness is a state of energy-in-motion in the mind. It radiates from our insides out and nurtures new growth to replace constant, tiny deaths," he said. "Mirror neurons and whatnot."

"Perhaps our love is like Einstein's spooky action at a distance," I said.

"Quantum entanglement?"

"When we came together, I felt spacetime shiver."

"That's sweet, darling," he said, and gave me a kiss.

He treated me to expensive brunch at an upscale concept diner in an refurbished old boxcar. He kept making prolonged eye contact with me and smiling, like he was looking for the way into my mind.

"What makes you happy?" he said, peering over the coffee cup in his hand. "I want to know how to make you happy."

"Nothing, no one, not even you, my pet," I said, feigning playfulness in hopes of pleasing him, at least to meet his kind gesture halfway.

Suddenly I panicked: I realized I had been so hungover the previous morning, I had forgotten to take the pill. He offered to escort me to Planned Parenthood and pay for Plan B. After flipping through pamphlets in the waiting room, I considered a more permanent solution.

I told the woman at reception I had no income, which was essentially true, so they wouldn't charge me for the visit—just a $20 copay on the device, which Marcel covered. I said he should wait in the nearby Starbucks. When finally I was seen, I had the doctor, a kindly, petite woman, insert a copper IUD inside me. The cramping from the insertion felt like being punched in the cervix with spiked brass knuckles.

I had expected nothing, but there he was in the lobby, holding a calla lily he'd picked out for me at a nearby bodega. I knew that I loved him then, but kept it to myself. I felt lightheaded from the procedure. My abdomen felt hollowed out as my cervix throbbed with piercing pain. He took me back to his place and ordered dinner for us both while I lit up a joint and smoked it on the fire escape outside his kitchen window.

He crawled out onto the fire escape and took a hit.

"I'd like you to meet my family," he said.

On his phone he opened a photo album called *Familie*. There was a picture of Marcel with his parents and two sisters in ski suits, smiling, in the Swiss Alps; another, the family in matching linen smocks atop the backs of camels outside Tangier.

"*Guten Tag*," I said to his phone, and we stoned-giggled.

My internal world and external reality oscillated around one another like two black holes. He'd lived, really lived, whereas I thought I had squandered so much time in my states of metaphysical egress. Ashamed I'd been nowhere in comparison, it occurred to me then that I had no perspective outside certain limitations. I thought perhaps he was my ticket out. Maybe we would get married and travel together. Maybe I'd get dual citizenship and move to Europe.

I fell asleep in his bed for the rest of the afternoon and dreamed uneasily. In the welter of a nightmare, everything I had ever been ashamed of, wanted not to be seen by others, was on display. Every single person I knew was laughing at me. Every single thing I had written down and torn up, or typed and deleted, still existed, somewhere, and some maligner had made it public. Every coincidence I had been pleased, moved, inspired by, had been staged to lure me to reactionary foolishness to be consumed by the cruellest of cynics. Every pleasant surprise turned out to have been an act of pity, merciful gestures reserved for times the gaze would bore of its squirming subject. Of course none of that was true. I had to know that. I got up, stripped down, and went to take a shower.

I stood over his unmade bed as I toweled off. He'd gotten into bed, naked, waiting for me to emerge clean. Black curls fanned out from the amorous core toward the twin peaks of his hip bones in a perfect isosceles triangle. The plush center of his mouth pouted a heart-shape. His chest hair rung neatly around the pink fleshy areolas. His smile stretched so broad across his face I swore I could see the skull behind it. His irises, a blue-grey like poppy seed, complete with that opiate effect, flecked with golden streaks like a marble.

My makeshift structure of pride caved in at once and, through tears, I explained to him that I was about to be homeless, and he invited me to move in with him. I told him he was insane, but immediately agreed.

I awoke drenched in cold sweat. It was my twenty-fifth birthday. The sun was rising behind the skyline across the East River, the wind was strong and getting colder, the streets were alight with traffic and bodies on their way to earn their living. I checked my phone. Marcel had called from Tanzania and left a voicemail. He said he may not be reachable for the next couple of days, but that he loved me very much.

He may have loved me but he could never understand the comings and goings of my fickle mood disorder, those disparate bouts of hopelessness. He could not save me, try as he might, from wandering off like a sleepwalker on those unexplained trips to some dreary harbor in my head where I would look into the abyss, waiting for I don't know what. But I wanted him to cultivate me into womanhood, into wife material, like

I was an empty plot of land, fertile but without life of my own. I couldn't stand to disappoint him, but in the shelter of his affection I didn't know what to do with my pathological thinking but to hide it, until I could no longer discern which of what I did or said was authentically me or the better me I fabricated for his sake.

Being left behind with my nothing of a life felt intolerable. I could not be present in the present. When depression took hold, like it had since Marcel's departure, I had a trick to elude the concerns of loved ones: an inverted disappearing act, like a black hole dying and imploding. Unwilling to join the day-world, I fell asleep again.

Consciousness hit me again in the afternoon. I dressed myself in a clinging black top, sheer enough that my nipples showed subtly with no bra underneath; black jeans, black boots; and Marcel's charcoal tweed sports coat. My hair was long, dark, bleached toward the tips in a grungy gradient. I had made all sorts of revisions to my appearance, obsessed with products, always another fashionable façade to cover for a failing authentic self.

On cigarette number three and with no writing accomplished, I felt an exhilarating impulse to burn it all. I slipped his electric shaver into the pocket of his jacket and climbed the stairs to the roof. I undressed completely. Every nerve seized up, every square inch of my skin smacked raw by the wind. I grasped bundles of hair and, piece by piece, sheared my head.

I redressed, descended the stairs, walked out the building onto the street towards Hotel Delmano, a bar several blocks away where my friend would be working that night. I felt all eyes on me, but quickly remembered I was nobody to everybody I passed.

I put out a cigarette and went inside, dusting ice off the shoulders of his coat. Misha was behind the bar. She slow clapped for me, then proceeded to ply me with liquor. The other patrons regarded me with what I perceived as quiet awe, like I was a great artist they thought they ought to have recognized. But I felt nothing. I might as well have been nowhere at all.

A couple of drinks down, then back outside for another cigarette. Wet snow clung to my eyelashes, promptly melted, then driveled across the shelf of my cheekbone. A group of us were slouched smoking under the awning, trying to avoid the sleet—"No, it's not, it's hail," I heard someone protest. Fielding advances with cigarette held in teeth, I assumed the calculated posturing that I reserved for warding off strangers on the street. I made believe that petulance could preserve my sense of dignity, no matter what low-frequency eye contact or crude remarks I was assailed with. I grimaced in the general direction of Midtown across the river, thinking everything was too ugly to be so iconic yet too iconic to be real. The great city's architecture had devolved into a dull, muddled concrete backdrop, all its majesty obscured by the piss-stain-and-cigarette-butt-snow and the dubious steam that rose ever up from the manholes and storm grates.

I could not continue gliding aimless along the karmic thermal of my existence. I killed more time than I spent feeling alive, hated myself so much despite so much love from such a good man. Self-loathing had become its own drab routine. I could risk no quality time alone with myself in between altered states, stuck with all my faculties fully functional yet so humiliatingly incapable of doing anything besides spending money I didn't have. At the ATM, my debit card yielded Insufficient Funds. It's not so much that I was stupid with money but that I was willfully in denial and devoid of self-discipline when depressed, impulsively choosing to spend on whatever would make me feel good short-term, a hand-to-mouth life.

Thinking, *Fuck it*, I took a taxi home, got out a block away from my place and ran to avoid payment, and went straight to bed. I rolled over onto my side, pulled the white duvet overhead and covered my body, my breasts squished beneath my wrists as I pulled my limbs into a fetal position. Eyes closed, a kaleidoscope vision looped incessantly until the black void at its core swallowed everything around it, washing all shape and color away. Patterns repeated obsessively, then evaporated from view, then were replaced by new fixations: the tension of consciousness in nauseatingly lucid resolution.

I reached over off the side of the bed for my notebook on the floor.

> *Being born was my first passive act. I let birth happen to me. I will die, which implies the inevitable as an activity I will participate in. Whether death happens to me or whether I happen upon death remains to be known.*

My heart still racing from ditching the cab fare, I could feel my pulse in my throat. It was cold in the apartment, so I wedged my hands between my thighs to warm them, then I smelled myself on my fingers. Under the covers I wriggled to generate heat. I remembered when I was a small child, too high-strung to fall asleep, I'd pretend I was swimming, kicking and churning my legs as if treading water in the sheets. I replaced my hand between my thighs and replayed in my mind the routine sex act between Marcel and me. His scent lingered in the sheets, mingling with the smell of my own sex, intensifying the euphoric sensory elevation. I tried not to think so much as feel—to articulate my body's sensations as I touched, rigorously, alternating vibration with firm fingertip pressure. It took surgical precision to get myself all the way there, each step on the way to the top as distinctive as sequential notes in a song changing from one key to another. On my back, I writhed, breathed hard, and shuddered softly. The feeling swelled up and rang outward from my pelvic core to the tips of my extremities.

A radiant little death for myself alone. *La pétite mort.* The transcendental climax of a deep vaginal orgasm is the closest I've ever come to believing in God.

The street lights glinted through the window opposite the foot of the bed, crystallizing the glare into myriad colors. In the dark calm, my thoughts raced like the cars that roared down the emptied streets late into the night.

I felt a curt vibration from within the tousled sheets. My friend Alix had sent me a nude self-portrait. In it she was hiding her pussy with a notepad boasting the Chateau Marmont letterhead, her name printed upon it under the words "In Residence." Scrawled below, in her immaculate script: "Wish you were here."

I met Alix in Montreal at my first-ever seedy loft party.

I'd moved into the college dorm downtown from small-town New England, where I'd grown up. I had long known I wanted to get out of America as soon as possible, so in school, I had become obsessed with studying French, a chosen pastime with which my peers were routinely perplexed. I wasn't sure what I wanted to do or who I wanted to be, but I knew I couldn't do or be what I wanted in the white-trash environs I'd known and hated. My parents didn't have the resources to help pay for college, but with the U.S.-to-Canadian-dollar exchange rate working in our favor, the federal student loans and financial aid money we qualified for would go farther. I'd be indebted for life, but at least it made a life possible.

On my way to the show I got lost, navigating uneasily between dilapidated industrial buildings in the dark until I saw smoke rising up behind one of them. I walked around back. There were train tracks on the other side of a chain-link fence that had been cut through and peeled back like a tin can. A two-storey factory that must have once relied on the trains for transporting its goods—whatever once-was industry had made its home here before such spaces became hot commodities for artists in search of cheap live/work spaces.

A bonfire had been shoddily kindled in the "backyard." The land was owned by the railroad company, but someone had put found, mismatched lawn furniture and raised garden beds there. A bearded man in a black brimmed hat and a leather jacket was situated across the fire.

"Please, sit down, there's beer inside if you want," he said. Harsh electronic music throbbed from the brick walls, which were painted where they hadn't been over-taken by leafy vines. There were bars on the large factory windows, and red, purple, and blue lights strobing inside. The man introduced himself as Dev and extended his hand to me. I accepted, said nothing. He smiled from inside his beard and stoked the flames, popping in and out of sight to collect twigs and planks. He didn't seem bothered I hadn't given him my name.

Some rosy-cheeked, Scandinavian-blonde young men with shaved heads were seated on a log, speaking amongst themselves. I tensed up but quickly readjusted myself to maintain composure, my shoulder blades softening down either side of my spine.

Dev said he had just returned from Mexico after a mountain retreat. He'd diverted from the script and gone off, on his own, in pursuit of peyote. He poked the fire. He went on about the long walks he'd taken along the border, through desert and brush, between one town or another, stepping nonchalantly between nations.

I drifted off and stopped paying attention for a while. A train approached and sounded off as it passed us. Dev stood with his back to the fire, waving at it with one hand, holding his hat against the gust it brought with the other.

Eventually, Dev said, he came across some locals and asked them where to find peyote—the only Spanish he'd learned—and they pointed him in the direction he wanted, just pointed off into the distance. Then he walked seven kilometers across a swath of desert, eyeing the terrain for the plant, until he came to another road. At that moment, a bus approached, a small contraption that shuttled fieldworkers between remote towns. When Dev boarded the ramshackle vehicle, with nothing to show for his exploit, the first thing he noticed was the Christ-nailed crucifix on the dashboard.

He lit another cigarette by the licks of his little conflagration. The noise of the train passing on the tracks behind us drowned out his voice, so we waited. Once the chugging and whirring had passed, Dev continued. He explained how his psychedelic spirit quest brought him to the wilds of Las Margaritas, where he found, at long last, his peyote. A local told him they call the strain he had found The Wizard. It was said to trigger a purge, the dark underside of the hallucinogenic experience.

Then the story was interrupted for a footnote. "Are you familiar with the mythopoetic imagination?" He said. My silence obliged him to continue talking as if I didn't know what he meant. "But I digress."

In or around Las Margaritas, Dev visited a shamaness. He'd found her on the Internet. She supposedly could locate a particular psychedelic mushroom. The shamaness lamented that 'The Voice' used to speak to her in a now-extinct native language until she introduced the mushrooms to voyaging gringos such as himself. Dev did not know what 'The Voice' meant—some sacred spirit-guide who communes with those who ingest the psychedelic plant, he gathered—but ever since, on walks through the wilds, the shamaness no longer would find the mushrooms, only dead animals. A felled coyote, a baby bird fallen from a nest, or the bottom of a half-eaten hare. She would collect them, counting them all omens. Depending how many she found along a certain path, she might never dare tread there again. The shamaness figured that to have sold the sacred mushrooms to tourists was to have betrayed the spirit that spoke through the plants, and as a result of this infidelity, she feared, her connection to the spirit had weakened.

"So what happened?"

"I left the next morning," he said. "Didn't want to bring the woman any more bad juju."

"I never realized all the trouble people go to for a trip, all the ceremony involved."

I'd never even taken a psychedelic drug, but I didn't say so. "Oh, yeah, it's huge in the world of high-functioning professionals right now," Dev said.

Another story: A friend of his, an investigative journalist, had become disillusioned by the media conglomerate that employed her after her report on the Iraq war had been partially censored. He said she traveled to Peru to do an ayahuasca ceremony. "And she did it. She found this mountain guru, who wore robes and had all these dogs." How did she get to Peru and locate this mountain guru? I wanted to know, but another train passed, so I didn't ask.

The fair blonde skinheads migrated inside the building. Dev's fire was dying down, so I walked inside too. Alix was standing in the back of the room, wearing a thick sweater, blue jeans, and ankle boots, with long dark hair hanging down the middle of her back. She was half-intently watching a gaunt, pained young man twist knobs and press keys on an old synthesizer. I recognized her from the dorm—she lived on my floor—but I'd been too afraid to approach her before. I moved towards her and, to my surprise, she looked up at me shyly and mouthed hello. She was so stunning in her plainness that it occurred to me at once she must intimidate most people into bashful silence, the way she did me.

When the noise/music was finished, I told her about the campfire stories, and she said she hadn't even known there was a backyard, so I took her out. Everyone else had left, but the embers from the fire were still smoldering. We sat and talked until it died down completely, then walked home together. We got lost for an hour or two on the way back to the dorm, but we had fun just walking and talking, like we could've kept on going until dawn.

Alix suffered a kind of anxiety different from mine. Her family was big on dignified self-restraint, teamed with healthy doses of discipline. She had been taught to keep any eccentricities under control inside of herself, not to burden others. The subterranean wellspring of anxiety would work its way to the surface in the form of severe panic attacks, during which she'd think she was dying.

She told me she was educated at a private school, where she dressed in uniform and everything. I felt hurt when she said she'd hated it. She'd been groomed to be the kind of well-heeled lady who was, to me, as magically unreal as a princess in a storybook. I always had lacked the ability to be consistently well-behaved. I remember being ejected from my first ballet class as a small child because I so had my heart set on freestyling the leaps and pliés I'd seen on TV that I flagrantly ignored the stern teacher's commands. If Alix's internal pressure culminated in a geyser burst every now and again in the form of an anxiety attack, my pressure valve was dysfunctional, chronically leaking signs of excess strife, constantly releasing streams of consciousness put to language—or, words set to the tune of my consciousness.

I could tell she was holding on to tension by the firm clench of her jaw. Her mandible was so elegantly defined, her posture so poised, she looked effortlessly graceful. She told me she felt like she barely got through each day without exerting a consistent baseline effort of control. I envied her discipline, the dignity with which she suffered. I too wished to suffer in style. To emulate her, I decided to devote focus to being gracefully present in my body: righting my posture, following my breathing—both of which, she explained, were her meditative practices, as well.

Manically wide-awake with excitement, Alix took me to her room to show me her art. She was going for a BFA in fine art with a specialization in photography. She shot 35mm film, incredible images printed in large-format and mounted on the wall. They were all photos of her, though sometimes she was unrecognizable, or her features shrouded in shadow. Alix throwing her long, fine hair back, captured in motion, backlit by sunlight through a window so the room around her disappeared, stripping the interior of its interiority, leaving only her figure and the view to outside. In this series she was naked except for an antique kimono left open. Her self-portraiture was gothically romantic, somewhere between still-life and cinematic, an abstraction of herself. She was the most herself in her work, I could tell. It was her as she was, in communion with her own gaze.

"I just developed the prints of a new series. They'll be ready tomorrow," she said, "but I don't think I can show them to anybody."

"Why not?"

"I don't know… I'm afraid they're too… exhibitionist."

"Isn't that kind of your thing, though?"

She looked at me blankly.

"Exhibitionism is only taboo to certain people under certain circumstances. Done well, it can be empowering, even just to look at."

She conceded that I was probably right.

"I'm just scared it will be taken the wrong way. That it will stop my career before it's even begun. Everything ends up on the Internet and then there's no taking it back, even if I regret it later."

"Will you at least show me?"

She looked at me tentatively, biting her bottom lip.

"Okay," she said. "I trust you."

We walked together from the dorm down to the art students' studio space the next day, one in a line of grey Brutalist buildings I never would've taken for a breeding ground for burgeoning artists. I liked the colorful parts of town, the Plateau where all the musicians lived; downtown was a drag, especially in the cold air which cast everything in grayscale.

She led me through nondescript hallways and up escalators and staircases. I followed her quietly, noting how disoriented I felt, focused intently on her, the long dark hair that hung down her back splayed over her worn-leather backpack, my nerves on edge at the thought she might turn down some corridor when I wasn't paying attention or slip into one of the many unmarked doors. We slipped into a darkroom where her photos were hanging like laundry from a clothesline.

She tapped one with her index. "They're dry," she whispered, and started taking them down and handing one after another to me.

One was her in a leather harness, binding herself with thick, scratchy-looking rope. The violence outstripped any first impression of sensuality implicit in her nudity.

Shadows blacked out her eyes, but her mouth was parted open like she was deeply focused on the act. Each photo had been snapped remotely and in succession. Her go-to way of shooting herself was to press the ball of her foot onto the button when she could see herself in the framing of the shot, as if she was inside of and in front of the camera simultaneously. She had to be disembodied in the moment to perform such a bodied practice. In each photo in the series she was closer to being immobilized. In the last photo her wrists were tied together. It was a shot of her with a horse-tail whip mid-stroke, about to begin flogging her perfect peach-shaped ass.

"You're like a female Robert Mapplethorpe," I said.

"Being called 'the female' *anything* is seriously reductive."

"I'm sorry, I didn't mean it that way."

"I know, but now you know."

She slid the prints and the negatives into her black leather portfolio onto the front of which she'd carved her initials, small, with an exacto knife. It was a grey afternoon. We walked to a sushi bar.

"Sushi in Montreal is shit compared to basically anywhere

on the West Coast," she said, "but anyway, I'm vegetarian, so it's just rice and cucumber to me."

"I hope you won't be disgusted while I slurp sashimi."

"I would never! I'm too focused on not being disgusting, myself. I'm really weird about eating in front of people."

Our first shared meal together, she held a hand in front of her mouth while feeding herself with the chopsticks she held with her other hand. I couldn't decide whether it would put her more at ease if I ate as comfortably as I would in any situation, or if it would be more polite to mirror her.

"Your anxiety about eating is rubbing off on me."

"I'm sorry!" She laughed at how serious she thought I was. "I have serious OCD. Like, I have anti-anxiety medication for it. But it puts me to sleep, so I rarely take it."

"Kidding, you're fine," I tried to reassure her.

She'd never so casually confessed to her mental illness to anyone before. What looked to me like effortless grace was a concentration of meticulous care fueled by a constant state of frenetic stress.

Riding the metro home, she rested her head on my shoulder. I put my arm around her. "You're my actual best friend," she said. "Seriously. You're the only one I feel like I can tell anything and everything." I wished we didn't have to part ways and go to our respective dorm rooms. I wished we could be together forever. I said nothing but "I love you," and hugged her goodnight.

I did not see her again for a month, and not for a lack of trying. When she finally met me for coffee, it was to announce that she had been admitted to another, better university, and was transferring. She invited me to her going-away party. I lied and said I couldn't make it.

I finished undergrad with a mediocre passing grade, moved to New York, and and began my new life of perpetual student-loan forbearance based on pitiful low income. Alix, meanwhile, graduated with honors from the more prestigious school, got into an illustrious artists residency program at an Italian villa, travelled freely for what seemed like months at a time, and presented work at a few prestigious small galleries. All the while our friendship had been relegated to email, an epistolary exchange as intimate as we'd been when we were together in person. I lied to myself that it was like we were never really apart. But her absence left a terrible void, nobody took her place in my life, no new confidante even came close. I stopped writing to her for months at a time sometimes, certain I was pathetic and that she only kept our correspondence going out of pity, or perhaps half-hearted sentimentality, or guilt-based responsibility for the life she'd left in the dust.

It was noon, the day after my birthday. I had not yet left my bed, I was so absorbed in rereading our latest correspondence.

To: Alix ---redacted--- {a-----@gmail.com}
From: C ---redacted--- {c-----@gmail.com}
12:59 am EST

Dear Alix,

███████████████████████████████████████
███████████████████████████████████████
███████████████████████████████████ I've been living outside of myself, like, composing my own character study, but I cannot tell if I'm one that has not yet been written, or if I am an utter cliché to my core. ████████████
███████████████████████████████████████
███████████████████████████████████████

x C

To: C ---redacted--- {c-----@gmail.com}
From: Alix ---redacted--- {a-----@gmail.com}
10:11 am PST

Dearest C,

I always think of you as writing your life slightly before or slightly after it happens, but always with the distance of time, even when that distance isn't there in this world.

x A

I felt a pang in my chest and knew I needed to see her, that nothing else mattered. How could I scrounge up the airfare? To augment my scheming, I stripped down to nothing and hot-boxed my bedroom.

To: Alix ---redacted--- {a-----@gmail.com}
From: C ---redacted--- {c-----@gmail.com}
5:55 am EST

Dear A,
It is February. SAD has debilitated me worse than allergies
did you in spring in Montreal the year we met. But,
my dearest friend, the distant promise of seeing you
again compels me to keep on living.

I want to write a story. I can't do it here, can't do anything
here anymore. I've got to come to the Southwest, as
you've beckoned me to before—perhaps like the last
surge of clarity and energy before a terminally ill person's
death, I am finally seeing things clearly. I'm coming,
somehow, and I would love to see you. I haven't quite
figured out where I'll be staying yet, so if you've got
any leads, I hope you'll be willing to help me out. I've
never been, but in my heart/mind I'm already there,
with you.
Love, C

To: C ---redacted--- {c-----@gmail.com}
From: Alix ---redacted--- {a-----@gmail.com}
9:25am PST

Dearest C,
Come here. You can stay with me. I cannot fucking
wait to see you. Buy the ticket and I'll meet you at the
airport.
Love, A

I remembered that Marcel had left a credit card behind for safekeeping. He'd given me the PIN and said I could use it in case of emergency while he was away. I took it from his sock drawer and used it to buy a one-way ticket. I packed as many clothes and toiletries I could fit into his gym duffel bag and used his credit card again to take a taxi to the airport. I texted her that I'd be at LAX in about six hours.

At airport security, I opted out of the body scanner and stood aside, nervously, while TSA agents called, "Female opt-out!" without the sense of urgency I anxiously craved. I had been horrified by the introduction of the "naked scanners" in my Bush-era teenagehood, back when the TSA was a new abomination. Waiting barefoot alongside the swiftly moving line, I considered maybe the scanner wasn't a cancer-ray-bombarding violation of human dignity, because nobody else seemed to think so. They just walked on through, raised their arms, moved on. But I had already made a statement of dissent, and I was clinging to that ego boost not to break down crying.

I had never been on a plane before. I made my way through the narrow aisle into economy, fumbling with my carry-on as I shuffled through in search of my seat. I wore denim cutoff shorts, black leather combat boots, a sweatshirt I felt comfortable in because it was too big for me and made me feel small, and a beanie that covered my new crewcut. The plane felt so much smaller on the inside than it looked. My mind went blank but for a heightened awareness of the compact space around me. Many faces appearing then disappearing. Stuffing their things into the overhead compartments. Families in tourist paraphernalia traveling together; men in suits traveling alone.

As the plane accelerated for liftoff, my body started to shake involuntarily. I was bawling, my face was drenched, the people sitting beside me were looking at me. "What have I done what have I done what have I done what have I done?" I hyperventilated. Once the plane reached high enough elevation, finally a flight attendant handed me a paper bag to "Breathe slowly in and out," she said. "Deep breaths, now."

I finished my second mini bottle of complimentary airplane *vino*. The past was irrelevant now that I was flying over all the flyover states on my way to the paradise city. The pilot's crackled voice told us to look over the right wing, because we were passing the Grand Canyon. I had the window seat. I got a good look at it.

I slipped in and out of consciousness until the plane landed at LAX. I let my body and luggage be volleyed into the fray of people in a heightened anxious state, catching connections and shuttles to the surrounding sea of parking lots. The highways wound around the place like an arcane fortress. Immediately upon stepping out into the battering daylight, I was suffused with a lightness, an unfamiliar sense of presence, like I'd been reanimated from frigid stasis. Overwhelmed and surrounded by an orderly chaos of cars, I watched in a daze as Alix, driving a vintage convertible, pulled into the pick-up lane. I threw my bag into the backseat and jumped over the door into the passenger's seat. We embraced as the cars honked furiously, impatient to take our place. I was so happy to see her, nothing else mattered. Then, in an instant, she maneuvered the stick-shift and the car lunged forward through a tight gap in the flow of traffic.

The glaucous golden-hour light cast the world in soft focus as we inched along the highway. We split off the highway and onto the surface streets, following signs for Venice, and before long we were surrounded by barefoot tourists and the commercial kitsch lining the glistening Pacific Ocean. We pulled over at a café that she liked, ordered coffee, and found an inconspicuous setting in which to light up a joint. Every new thing presented an opportunity for me to attach meaning to it. I was awake in these strange surroundings, gawking open-mouthed at it all.

We saved the rest of the joint and walked down to the beach. I stripped to my underwear and ran into the waves. One wave, much taller than me, smacked me in the face and swept the sunglasses right off my nose. I looked back at Alix and screamed with joy.

At sunset, we lay on a Mexican blanket spread on the hood of her car, quiet, watching the smog turn colors until the sky became darker, the air cooler. She put the roof up and drove us toward Hollywood.

As we idled on the I-10 West, she explained that she'd inherited the car from her father. I could smell gas fumes as the nubile contraption cruised languidly along like it clearly wasn't meant to. Her little convertible was difficult: its sputtering engine occasionally lurched us forward when she switched gears, and I felt every bump in the road in my bones.

The significance of my relationship to Alix had grown, in my mind, wildly out of proportion to reality. I'd idealized our reunion so romantically, but a baseline of slight awkwardness set into our silences. For all our epistolary exchanges in the years since I'd seen her face-to-face, I didn't really know her as well as I thought. I wanted to be so close, as if we inhabited an eggshell, leaving no room for formalities, only pure unadulterated intimacy. But everything I'd fantasized seemed preposterous now. I had idealized and objectified her as would a teen boy uncomfortable in his skin, too intimidated by her beauty and poise to look her in the eye. I steeled and commanded myself to get over it.

"You're doing me the biggest favor," I said. "I don't know how I can ever repay you."

"Don't be ridiculous," she said. "I'm so happy to see you!"

Then, again, an uncomfortable silence. I squirmed, fidgeted, looked at myself disapprovingly in the rear-view mirror. It was only a matter of time, I thought, until she became disappointed with who I really was or had become in our time apart, until she saw me for the loser/mooch/burden I was.

"I'm so proud of you for leaving, for coming out here," she said, surprising me.

"Thanks. But I feel like I'm a terrible person. I didn't tell Marcel I was going away."

"On the contrary, I think it was really brave and badass to leave like you did," she smirked, "but maybe I'm a terrible person, too."

"You are the best person on the planet."

"It's always unfortunate when your self-actualization results in a few casualties, but it's also more or less inevitable," she said. "Sometimes you've just got to do what's best for you. Everyone's a little selfish sometimes."

Driving east through town was jarring. Zombie-like beings pushed silver shopping carts overflowing with hot garbage, dressed in ragged clothes several sizes too large and roaming streets lined with tents; tarp-covered makeshift structures pitched alongside the highway on-ramps strewn with fast-food trash, fenders, grills, hubcaps. The air was so dry, I had a runny feeling in my sinuses and the iron-tinged deep-throat taste of an oncoming nosebleed. At least shade brought relief from the heat, unlike in humid New York summertime.

"Love the new look, by the way," she said.

"I think my scalp is sunburned," I said.

The car labored up the narrow winding streets, up steep curves dense with forest, until we arrived at the house.

"It's so beautiful," I said, "like a man-made wilderness for a movie set."

"Just a fortuitous collaboration between man and nature," she said. "Drought-tolerant landscaping is *de rigueur* now. But the Canyon gets much greener when it rains. God, I wish it would rain."

Little lizards ran around our feet as we headed up the dusty walkway, impressive spiderwebs were draped between the banisters and steps on the old wooden staircase that led up to the front porch. I felt like an intruder, but couldn't help but gawk at them, mildly repulsed but too in awe not to admire the creatures up close. Old-growth oaks loomed between the house and the road, and the tangle of shrub and vine sat so dense on the grounds that the road seemed to disappear. It felt like we were far removed from civilization.

"A fifteen-minute walk down that road will take you to the Country Store," Alix said, "if you need anything."

"I feel like this place isn't even in LA," I said. "It's so idyllic. So far removed from Hollywood, and yet it's right there at the foot of these hills. And I don't think I've ever seen so many homeless people in my life."

She narrowed her catlike eyes, looked ahead in silence for a moment.

"I can tell already that the economic inequality here is insane."

"I've never thought about it that way. But if it bothers you that much, I don't know how you can stand living in New York," she said.

"Well, I couldn't stand it. That's why I'm here."

"True," she said. "I could never live there. I love New York, but it's like the epicenter of apathy. I was taking the Manhattan-bound L train one afternoon, and I saw this girl—she was dressed like an uncanny union of real money and taste, with a Céline bag slung on her forearm. I wanted to take her picture, so I followed her out of the 8th Avenue stop and onto 14th Street, but I lost her. In the middle of the sidewalk, there was a young black man passed out in his wheelchair. He was an amputee, and the pant legs of his sweatpants were tied off at where his knees should've been. He'd pissed himself. I watched people come out from the subway and just walk in a wide arc around him, like he wasn't there. I thought he might need help, but what could I do for him? I couldn't photograph him, though. I thought he deserved at least that shred of dignity."

"I don't think that kind of apathy is unique to New York," I said.

"Maybe," she said, "but maybe it's pointless to try to compare. LA is completely different."

I looked around the house in quiet awe. "So, you live here?"

"No, I live in an apartment in Echo Park. But this is the house I grew up in. Part of the time, at least. It was my father's. Can't be bothered with managing guests on AirBnb or anything, but I can't bear to sell it, either," she said.

Inside, the house smelled like the pages of an old book. Shelves built into the walls of the entryway were filled with them. She showed me where to put my things, and said I could shower and change. She could go first, I offered; I needed to decompress.

I watched her undress and admired her shape, her long hair shiny but unkempt, her skin immaculate, an even wash of French-vanilla upon a tender canvas. Breasts fuller than mine; nipples smaller, perkier, pinker than mine. The shape of her arm was even more delicate than mine, her posture upright but soft, the curve of her lower back a sublime arch, her ass plush as a peach and almost perfectly heart-shaped, catching diffuse light in its cusp. Worried I'd make her uncomfortable, I stopped staring and opened my sloppily packed duffle bag and began to undress, too, wishing for something light and pure to wear. I settled for a white button-down shirt, oversized enough to cover to my thighs, that smelled like Marcel; I'd pulled it from the dirty laundry hamper and stuffed it in my bag before leaving. Alix offered me a pair of handcrafted espadrille slippers. Our feet were the same size.

I studied the eclectic objects strewn gracefully around the house: gothic crucifix and rosary on the coffee table, hand-painted wooden boxes filled with camera parts, antique candlesticks, lighters and pipes. Each thing I honed in on seemed to have something eerie, uncanny, or antiquarian about it. A desk with a deeply aged leather insert, like what you'd imagine in a proper gentleman's study, was there in the common area. "Feel free to take this as your work space," she said as she gave me a brief tour. The surface was sparsely decorated with a small, handmade ceramic ashtray, a table lighter, a brass lamp, a notepad with the Chateau Marmont letterhead, and dried red roses in a vase perched atop a leather-bound Dictionary of the Occult.

Fresh out of the shower, Alix put on a white cotton T-shirt and high-waisted blue jeans she'd well worn through. I noticed the upturned corners of her eyes when she smiled, and the soft tan freckles on the apples of her cheeks from having driven home in the sun with the top down, and the perfect pindot of a mole at the base of her throat that she wore like a pendant. Suddenly I understood: To leave well enough alone is the look. She embodied her body fully, and that's what made her so gorgeous, so elegant, so unlike how I felt about myself. Yes, she had won the genetic lottery, but it was something else that made her otherworldly: that rich-girl aura of innate confidence and inalienable security. She epitomized natural beauty. Her lean body was simply what she had to show for her good health. She was enviably un-fucked-with. Maybe she put some lipstick on now and again. Besides that, she was just how she was meant to be. She conducted herself with enviable effortlessness.

It occurred to me then that grace is being at ease within oneself. She did not suffer the same frenetic anxiety that I did of having been raised in an unstable environment, by which I mean I chalked our differences up to class. Maybe what I perceived as elegance was in truth the embodiment of financial stability.

I ignored the weight and stress of money that bore down relentlessly on my skeleton. We were connected, bonded by a friendship that transcended not just distance and class, but logic itself. I complimented the artwork she had strewn about: some technicolor photos her father had taken in the '60s, blown up and framed, and some original figure drawings and erotic watercolors—some by friends of hers, some by old friends of her father's, she said.

The next day, Alix insisted she show me around the city. She drove us down Laurel Canyon Boulevard into Hollywood and then toward the Eastside, angling around the network of villages connected by highways masquerading as a city. I'd watch out the window as she drove along the incongruity of buildings and signage, the dilapidated industrial expanse, thoroughfares abandoned with the sole exception of its denizens, and then rows of abandoned storefront real-estate with signage so generic it all looked like part of a movie set. We passed a Vinyl and Linoleum Floor Warehouse that had a row of tents and tarps and piles of garbage piled up alongside it, a micro-neighborhood on the sidewalk. A massive neon sign in red on the side of a building by the highway read DREAM CENTER. It could've been a branch of the Church of Scientology or a discount mattress depot for all I knew, but the way the sign shone over the highway signalled something ominous.

There was a man in a red polo shirt waving a red flag at the mouth of a parking lot like a horse's tail swatting at flies, his dewy brow furrowed into a scowl to discourage sunlight from reaching his eyes. Beggars weaved around cars stopped in traffic and rapped their knuckles on the car windows of anyone who mistakenly made eye contact. There were tents and strung-up tarps lining the thoroughfares, especially densely populated under the overpasses, populated with the ragged lonesome. Lost boys and girls climbed up the embankments to pick through fast food containers discarded by passing cars.

There was no charm in any of it. Nothing about Los Angeles enchanted me the way the idea of it had. I couldn't help but think I was alive at the wrong time—or, at exactly the right time to see through the previous generation's debauched idealism. Nothing was sacred. Elliott Smith's face was painted on a mural on the side of Floyd's Barbershop on Sunset Boulevard, and just beside it was a bus-stop bench advertising Courtney & Kurt Real Estate. On the bench, surrounded by garbage bags packed with urban detritus, another lost soul slept off his existence.

Alix remarked that the tent cities in LA were "nothing" compared to the refugee camps in Europe. She'd been on a train from London to Paris not long ago, hoping to photograph the makeshift village in Calais populated by refugees. These were not addicts and mentally ill people like the ones on LA's streets, she said, but doctors, lawyers, teachers, husbands and wives and their children separated by artificial boundaries they'd been forced across by violence, adrift and denied the dignity of a destination. The train she was on came to a stop midway under the frigid Channel. There were people walking through the tunnel trying to cross from France to the U.K. The train was held up for two hours while border patrol officers "processed" the refugees and filed them out to a camp where they'd live in a holding pattern for months.

The globe wasn't turning on an axis, it was caught in a shame spiral. I found her well-intentioned, well-informed concern for the refugees a bit phony, despite myself, seeing now first-hand that she epitomized the word *lifestyle*. But I despised the loadedness of the word *lifestyle*. They say Californians invented *the lifestyle*. It's weighted with so much consumerist bullshit, but to a writer or artist I could see now it was part of the creative process. I felt a strong impulse to protect and defend this new lifestyle at all costs, as if at any moment someone would find me out as the fraud I was and rob me of it. The center of the universe is everywhere and nowhere within it. I had no sense that I truly belonged anywhere, which allowed me to feel at home everywhere I went. So much eluded one at all times: all of the crushing, oppressive detail that goes into any one thing, a bottomless nesting doll of atoms upon atoms down to the purest of pure sub-stance; the triviality of our conflicts over various degrees of transaction; the human senselessness of focusing on any one thing and not the millions of more important things. There was no winning.

"Awareness doesn't have to come with guilt," Alix said.

"Easy for you to say. You're one of the chosen ones. Wasn't your mother one of Joni's 'Ladies of the Canyon'?"

She rolled her eyes and smiled.

"Money really doesn't matter nearly as much as you like to think."

"Of course it does!" I laughed.

"At least give me the credit that I know something about what it means to live the artist's life."

It was a fair point. "You've got these limiting beliefs," she went on. "They only hold you back from aligning with your authenticity."

"Really," I deadpanned.

"First of all, you don't have to be rich and stable and in control to be a great artist."

"Listen, I was working days at a coffee shop and nights on webcam to support myself while I was interning. And you were—where, again? London? Paris?"

"You know, I think all your self-righteous class consciousness is a copout."

"Wow! Tough love."

"I'm not saying I haven't enjoyed privilege and good fortune. But if being an artist is a privilege, it's one that must be earned to be real, and it's accessible to any talented, hardworking person."

"I'm sorry to say this, because I love you, but you really don't get it."

"No, yeah, I get it. I know we've had different experiences. But I'm honestly a little jealous of you. I admire you so much for working hard all on your own to make it happen for you."

"That astonishes me! Besides, I don't even know what I do, or what I'm doing here, besides loving being with you."

"Well, you have everything you need to thrive creatively here. Start thriving!"

I hugged her for what felt like a beat too long.

"I will need a car, though."

"Take mine anytime you want."

"I can't drive a stick."

"I meant my other car. The Prius."

"Of course it's a Prius."

"It's all yours if you want it. I'm really into the convertible right now."

"Must be nice!" I reclined and clasped my hands behind my head.

"Want to drop acid later?" she said.

"You know—? I've never taken acid before."

"Shut up."

"No!"

"We're doing it."

"No pressure or anything."

"Do you want to do it or not?"

"Obviously."

We got home around sundown. She said we'd have to skip dinner if we wanted the full effect. She retrieved an old wooden jewelry box from the lofted bedroom and opened it. It was lined in blue velvet and contained immaculate little plastic baggies of fine powders and smiley-face tabs.

"I've got shrooms, too," she said, "in the freezer. Help yourself."

I was afraid. Insanity was as much an adjunct of myself as my shadow. I conceived of my brain as a soluble thing. Too chickenshit to violate that precarious balance, I had never so much as tried a bump in my life. As a teen, I was straightedge. A soft pseudo-punk screaming alone in the woods. I smoked my first joint in my freshman year of college. In New York, I rarely got my hands on decent weed, and anyway was too high-strung for it. But here, now, with Alix, I thought, what the hell.

We were sitting on the back porch. The sun was soon to set. Mosquitoes out for blood swarmed by the treeline. We each took a single tab on our tongues. While we waited for it to hit us, she scattered blankets, throw pillows, and meditation cushions across the living room floor. I lit incense and candles. She arranged a collection of crystals on the coffee table in the center of the room, "so we'll have a good, easy trip," she said, and I paced, excited but cagey. The succulents and cacti around the house were as big as me, oversaturated with color. One looked flat and wide and shaped like a paddle jutting out slim white spikes. I imagined breaking an arm off and using it as a paddle to spank myself. I cringed. I took a hit of her dad's retro Chihuly bong and sat on the teakwood patio furniture decorated with handwoven Kilim pillows and spider-woven webs. I filled and refilled my handmade ceramic cup with the Mountain Valley Spring water that was delivered weekly to the house in large glass jugs.

Alix and I sat opposite one another in half-assed lotus pose on the cushions. The sun had gone down. We looked at each other by candlelight. Her hair cascaded over her shoulders. She was wearing a silk kimono. I was wearing an oversized sweater and denim cut-offs. Her eyes grew in size, then shrank down, then grew larger again.

"You look so tiny!" she said, "Look at your tiny shaved head in all that sweater!"

The candlelight flickered on her hair and the light reflected warped playfully before my eyes. Again her eyes looked bigger, then smaller, and I couldn't help but laugh.

"Let's have some music," she said and walked very cautiously around the cushions, over to the record player, and put on an Ethiopian jazz record.

In a moment of boldness, I trained my eyes on her in fine detail: the texture of her, the faint lines and pores of her skin, the minor cosmetic imperfections—the front teeth slightly off, the narrowed cat-eye mischief in her conspiring look. I'd observed her closely enough this time that what I was seeing ceased to be Alix at all. For a moment, my curiosity muscled in front of my care for her feelings, obscuring in my view her separateness from me.

I had lost all sense of time passing. I checked my phone, which I had been avoiding since I'd arrived.

"Oh my god."

"Is it him?" Alix said.

I was scrolling through and rapidly scanning all the missed calls, texts, and voicemails, my eyeballs frenetic, darting to and fro in their sockets. I began to hyperventilate, and she shushed me and took the phone out of my hand.

"Deal with it later. You're fine."

We were rolling and crawling and loafing around on the pillows on the floor for what felt like a minute, then Alix looked at the old cuckoo clock and said "It's already been an hour since we started tripping!" We cuddled and laughed at existing and passed a joint back and forth. She grabbed a box of colored pencils and a sketchbook and started to draw. "You want one?" I said I needed a minute. Just to sit and feel.

"It feels like when you've been swimming in the ocean too long and you can still feel the waves passing through once you've dried off and laid down on the sand."

"It's a warm-and-fuzzy feeling."

She rose and began a sinuous dance, moving her arms like a swan in flight.

"Dance with me."

"I look like an awkward loser next to you."

"Okay, first of all, your self-esteem needs a serious adjustment."

I gasped feigning insult.

She looked me in the eyes, I looked her in the eyes, I leaned in closer, she said "Your pupils are super dilated, whoa," and I backed up, collapsed in defeat, rolled onto my back and stared at the ceiling.

She insisted we go out for a walk and I, feeling suddenly small and fragile, like I would be crushed by the weight of the atmosphere were I to leave the house, reluctantly followed. We walked up the road and looked at the other houses, the cars parked in front of the houses. I lit up and laughed aloud; they looked like toys: doll houses and Barbie pickup trucks. I jumped up onto the ledge of the back of the pickup truck and Alix whisper-yelled "NO!" as I swung myself up onto the bed of the truck and fell onto my back. We made stunned eye contact, waiting for a thick moment for an alarm to sound, for trouble to suck the air out of our sails. But it didn't, we both laughed, I climbed down, and we walked to the Canyon Country Store. I didn't know what time it was, but The Store was still open. It was an authentic relic of a certain iconic hippie-rock-and-roll brand of Americana kitsch, but it was also just a store. Once, I had been vaguely impressed upon by the stories, the long-gone legacy of the place, just like many other places that were demystified, too, upon my entering them. Reality rarely if ever satisfied my expectations. Like a child, I forged most expectations in my overexuberant imagination.

The usual mire of my waking thoughts suddenly ran clear, and delight percolated to the surface like spring-water gurgling up, dissolving depression's vice-grip on my internal monologue. This was a sneering voice that I now realized had plagued me for as long as I could remember, like the mind-control parasite that eats and replaces the tongue of a fish. The voice was something apart from my own, an intruder violating my soul.

In a sudden epiphanic deluge, I realized that that which connects us exists outside the world of language, that the way we love is at once too basic and too elaborate to articulate. If it can be reduced to language, it can be reduced, like a chemical compound, to a purer substance, and what I'm talking about, I could not bear to learn this love was not its own elementary substance; it was the only thing I refused to question.

The time between each euphoric waves' cresting grew longer, or I was coming down and only beginning to regain a regular sense of time.

"You've been quiet for awhile," Alix said.

"Sorry," I said. "It's amazing. I don't have the vocabulary for it."

"There's a lot of writing out there about the psychedelic experience. Aldous Huxley wrote *The Doors of Perception*. And then there's Terence McKenna."

"Any women?"

"You know—? I don't know."

"I think... I don't want to read anybody else about this. I want to keep it pure."

The cabin had a lofted second floor that Alix had set up as a bedroom, just a mattress on the floor. That's where I slept. When she stayed over, as she did the night we took acid, we shared the mattress. I wanted to entwine my limbs with hers but kept a platonic distance.

In the morning she made us green smoothies and I made the coffee. We sat quietly together with our work for a few hours until she made eye contact and said, "Lunch?" and I narrowed my eyes like I'd just heard something mind-blowing and said, "Yeah," and we got in her convertible and went to Café Stella.

The dining room at Café Stella was *en plein air* with ceiling fans despite the lack of actual ceilings, and a black-and-white checkered floor and lacquered wicker chairs. The clientele was seeing and being seen. The Côte de Boeuf cost $100.

I just wanted to commune with good vibes all fucking day. Those heavenly doldrums. With her, anything would do. I wasn't afraid not to work for a change. Time was free.

"I understand now how great art is made," I said, and she squinted at me and nodded knowingly.

She held one hand in front of her mouth while she raised her fork to her lips with the other. She appeared to be less anxious about eating in front of others than she had been in college, but still made the same modest gesture.

"Have you thought about writing a screenplay?" she asked.

"Never. I don't know the first thing about screenwriting."

"Oh, it'll be easy for you. Every other asshole in LA does it. There's a book on the basics somewhere at the house."

"What makes you think I could write anything worth watching?"

"Have you seen the shit people watch now?"

"No. I haven't had cable television since I left for college."

"Neither have I. But TV and film still reign over the zeitgeist. It's just migrated to the Internet."

"But I don't have a story to tell."

"You do. It's why you're here."

"Like, on Earth?"

With a carefree laugh, she waved her hand in front of my face.

"Yes! Earth to Calla! Are you with me?"

When the waiter brought the bill, she handed over her credit card without so much as a glance at the total. I made eye contact with her, my mouth agape.

"Don't even think about it," she said.

Alix did the best and worst things with equally graceful nonchalance: smoke a joint on Sunset Boulevard while making nice with the bouncer outside of the bar in front of Café Stella; exhale a plume that, for an instant, consumed her black lacquered, perfect oval fingernails.

When we got home, she took her avant-garde fashion shitkicker boots off standing up, one at a time, and put them in the proper place before sinking into the couch for a rest. She was braless under a clinging ribbed-knit silk shirt, satiny hair rippling over the curb of her collarbone. I looked through the books for the one about screenwriting.

Another old book stood out to me: *The Hero With A Thousand Faces*. I picked it up. The narrative structure was familiar, a celebration of the harrowing and legendary exploits of classical phallic power. The divine call, the hero's response; the hero transported into some alternate reality that reroutes him, by the myth's end, back to the beginning—caveat: enlightenment. Women only ever appeared as a distraction or temptation, or a victim, or a widow, or something else entirely surreal, a goddess. And the double-standards! What real-life heroine would not be debased by critics male and female alike for attempting half the sleights necessary to parallel the heroism of a supernaturally buff, supernaturally privileged, cocksure male hero? Mythology never appealed much to me, as I am not enthralled by any ethos that demeans my existence. Also on the bookshelf were jagged chunks of rose quartz and amethyst, and an art-deco brass tray holding a stack of miniature firewood. ("It's palo santo," Alix said.)

I found the book she'd been talking about and flipped through it. It said *my* movie had to be a story only I could tell from my unique, authentic perspective. Write what you know, it advised. Then it explained formatting, time per page, dialogue, structure.

Storytelling through cinema was mysterious to me, as a person who'd fetishized the prestige and cultural capital of writing great literary prose. For all I had written in and about my life in New York, none of it brought me the kind of closure, fulfillment, or cathartic release I was looking for. I lived without expressing, gagged by the feeling of never being the right kind of alone, never far enough that someone couldn't hear me through a wall if I screamed. The claustrophobic environment deformed all moments of peaceful solitude into a terrifying, existential loneliness, the understanding that just because I'm physically close to someone doesn't mean they care, doesn't mean they'd stop to help if I'd been attacked on the street, doesn't mean they would've noticed if I hadn't left my apartment for weeks. My mind hadn't had the space to expand from the confines of a paperback cover to the grandiose enigma of film.

Genuine solitude was more accessible in LA. Time seemed to pass differently, too. Invisible and undercover forces seemed to move time forward, not the seasonal sequence I was used to. My memory struggled to register how much time had passed since I had left Marcel without a word by way of goodbye. Without a marked change in weather, nailing down the time and place of a particular memory was like giving directions without landmarks. The isolation was pleasant, though, if only because I spent more time outside than I ever had in New York. What felt like isolation in one city was luxurious privacy in another. Being alone in the Canyon felt safe in a way that satisfied my primal instincts, like having my back to the wall. I languished in the rose-gold light of the magic hour, wondering how Italo Calvino would've caricatured LA now were it one of his *Invisible Cities*: the oppressive sprawl of strip malls, the mislaid suburban-style housing, the congested arteries of the highways...

I decided to give in to the abundance of my newfound circumstance, and began to write.

I had an idea that I could write an exegesis of my inner self and that way figure out what was wrong with me. I wrote diligently, falling into a daily routine: wake, write, coffee, write, eat, and by afternoon my racing thoughts and discomforting solitude would throw my equilibrium off. A storm brewed in my mind by two o'clock: too much to articulate inundating the fore of my mind all at once. So I'd smoke pot and lay in the hammock for an hour or two, withdrawing from all concern and powering down my perception. After resting the afternoon away I worked through the evening, compelled by a vertiginous unease in my gut, stopping only to satisfy bodily needs (eat/pee/masturbate).

I'd always found stream-of-consciousness prose to be alienating unless you're allowed to know the agonizing story of the years of festering obsession, fear, pride and shame that add up to insanity. I could dispose of my past, having not inherited any cultural nor monetary capital. Cultural capital is an analogue of actual money, I thought. Public recognition of my most private pastime would validate my existence to posterity. Being seen—read—would justify me. I'd create a beautiful byproduct of my inane suffering and self-absorption. Meaninglessness made the universe seem supple, like I could pull off whatever I wanted when I stopped believing in the rules, and negated the need for a reason to live. Whatever tethered my identity to myself had dissolved in the acid. Yet no worthwhile prose was coming of any of this. Whole days amounted to pages of meaningless rambling. I felt like an animal in heat who had missed out on mating season.

Not much changed about the landscape as weeks coalesced into months. California remained in drought. I longed for rain to break up the squalid atmosphere. Belligerent sunshine bore down on me with such a great pressure to live. I didn't have the appetite to fatten up my anemic personality by venturing out into the city or being a woman of the world, unlike Alix, who was a natural socialite. Night came and cooled my head. Colossal climate-change cataclysms, wildfires burning hundreds of arid acres, and the impending mega-earthquake all threatened the landscape beyond human control. We went about our days in static comfort as if nothing would ever change.

One night Alix came over and we opened up a bottle of mezcal, made unsweet margaritas, and listened to records. I chose *Broadcast and The Focus Group Investigate Witch Cults of the Radio Age*; she, *Colour Green* by Sibylle Baier. We sat together underneath a blanket and talked aloud to one another about the mechanisms of our internal worlds, the parallels between our life's great stories, the romance of our friendship. I felt we'd exceeded the presumed security of a sisterly reprieve, like we'd reached peak honeymoon phase without the sex.

I was telling her about my writer's block. The oppressive cheerfulness of the sunshine. The void my head was lost in.

"Try going on a detox," Alix said.

"What for?" I said.

"You know, toxins. So much pollution in LA. Also, drinking."

"Gotcha."

"I tried the candida cleanse for a few weeks," she said with consternation. "That was crazy."

"You had candida?"

"No, yeah, I don't know. Doesn't everybody?"

"I'm not sure."

"Well I felt better, I think. You have to cut out gluten, sugar, and fermented foods... garlic and onions... mushrooms, legumes... anything acidic, like tomatoes or vinegar... cruciferous vegetables... coffee and alcohol, too. But tequila and mezcal are okay."

"How's that?"

"I read somewhere that tequila is the most low-glycemic booze. It's made from the blue agave."

"You found a nutritional loophole? You're so brilliant."

"Shut the fuck up."

"My brilliant friend."

"Stop, you're the true genius."

"No, *you're* a genius."

"Okay we're both geniuses."

"As long as we agree."

I was as confused as ever between wanting her and wanting to be her. I felt so safe but I couldn't help but feel I was deeply in her debt, too indulgent, too precocious, too evasive, preoccupied in living my personal fantasy by virtue of Alix's hospitality. She was well-behaved, while I'd fidget, fuss over my posture, crack my bones, pick at my nails, anxiously run my hands through my hair, trying to settle on a natural pose to accompany the silence. My bones moved in tandem with or against each other; the connector on the left side of the head, where the mandible joins the skull, chafed and popped out of and back into place like the gears shifting on a bicycle chain. My body felt like a carapace of socially coded illusion, a shell with which I protected the weak and vulnerable inner self, who feels and wants and needs things.

"I'm so happy here. I'm so grateful to you," I said. "Now I just have to make some money."

"Don't worry so damn much. Trust that the universe has your back. I have this spiritual advisor who reads my cards and my numbers. She does it all. She always says we're each of us on this journey to become the most whole version of our true self."

I laughed. "That's *so* LA."

"No, I mean it. You create your own reality based on your belief in yourself. If you have a scarcity mentality, you won't get far. If you have an abundance mentality," Alix said, "the universe provides everything we want. We just have to trust it. And believe in ourselves."

I was about to say, "Isn't that like blaming the poor for their poverty when the real problem is systemic?" but I knew she'd know what to say to that, so I gave her the benefit of the doubt. Also, it's understandable that she wouldn't get it. She had never been close to falling out of grace with society due to insufficient funds. She hadn't had to flail pathetically to save herself from destitution. I couldn't say that, of course. She said I was house-sitting but really, I knew I was a lowly squatter in The House of Yes. Every time I remembered my unsaid debt to Alix, I felt our previous intimacy was nullified. She feels sorry for me, with my bad skin and bad credit and no friends, I thought obsessively. But then she would say something like, "Look at how much you write, you're prolific," and peer over my shoulder to steal a glance at whatever I'd scribbled. She believed in me, or at least she put it to faith that something good had to come of the sheer volume of words I committed to pages on any given day.

I depended on that validation.

"So, I got some good news today," she said. Her first solo show was opening at a London gallery in about a month. She'd have to leave town for a while. I was stricken nauseous with envy, but I congratulated her, hugged her, smiled for her.

On the streets of LA and every other city she'd visited in the last few years, she'd photographed destitute people, addicts (meth, heroin), the forsaken mentally and terminally ill populace scarcely acknowledged by society, all captured in black-and-white 35mm film. She was calling the collection *Among the Living*. A lot of people wanted to meet her and write about her work. She'd told me all about it well before I'd come barreling with my physical presence into her daily life. It almost felt like I'd been there with her.

"It's about alienation from life in the proximity of death, or the dehumanization of the sick and dying, or how swiftly we all become irrelevant to the world's machine-like movements, how lonely it is to be excluded from the routine transactions of many," she said. We kept talking as she began to pack a suitcase. She assured me I was welcome to continue in the luxurious solitude sequestered in the Canyon as long as I liked or needed. It was one of those nights I could not be close enough to the ground. It was the wrong night to mingle with strangers, but Alix wanted to party one last time before she left town. Sasha, a friend Alix hadn't introduced me to yet, came to pick us up. He was a stylist with a pretty mouth who slouched under layers of mono-chromatic designer clothing. Sasha came to get us in his boyfriend's black SUV and we headed to a party in the Hollywood Hills.

First thing Sasha did was lead us into the bathroom. The three of us filed in. We talked to one another in the mirror while Sasha pulled an Altoids tin out from his pocket, slid it open, his fingers manicured better than mine, and pulled out a baggie, shuffled some of the powder out onto the smooth flat back of the key he'd just unsheathed from the car's ignition, and breathed in deep. Alix had dabbled in some past life and was not so fond of it anymore. Sasha was something of a connoisseur. "He always has good shit," Alix said, and Sasha said, "I do shell out for premium." He drew a few lines for us on the ridge of the bathroom sink. I did a line and marvelled in the back of my mind as the self-serious ego took over.

"I'd like you to tell me who I'll be dealing with," I said.

"Just some industry bitches." He talked low and in quick spurts. "The house is André's."

"Who is André."

"The overdressed one."

"Everyone's overdressed."

"The one with the big teeth and the crow's feet."

"Haven't seen him."

"Don't worry girl. He'll see you."

As soon as we exited the bathroom and scattered like those particles into Sasha's scarred sinus cavity, I found myself standing beside someone handsome.

"You're a tough cookie, aren't you."

"Excuse me?"

"The way you carry yourself. I can tell."

"And you're—let me guess—an actor."

He laughed pretentiously. "She's smart, too." He was tall, with a flop of dark curls and very blue eyes. He had grandpa glasses on, with a colorful rope attached at the stems and draped back around his neck, so he could take them off and let them hang if he was vibing on low-fidelity vision. We sat on the ground, by the pool, close to one another.

"Who do you know here?" he asked me.

"A friend of a friend."

"Same," he said, sucking on a cigarette, blowing smoke into the dark light.

"Wanna one-card reading?" he said, reaching for his jean jacket pocket.

"Come again?"

He laughed at me again and took a tarot deck from the pocket.

"Pick a card. It'll be fun." He spread them out on the edge of the tile lip over the glowing pool.

I picked one just slightly off-center from the middle. He flipped the card over.

"Ten of Swords! Interesting."

"A deer speared through with ten swords. What's that supposed to say about me?"

"Overkill. This is you, intellectually, struggling with hyper-analyzing everything to death. But it's ten, meaning it's a hopeful card—you're about to begin a new cycle."

"So… I am presumably almost over this overkill phase."

"Righto, kid."

"Don't call me that."

I dropped the card on top of the splayed deck.

"So, what do you do?" he said.

What a question! I wished he'd asked more honestly: What do you contribute to the world? How do I judge your credibility, or gauge your value to my own motives? How do I know, as efficiently as possible, whether to dismiss you?

"I'm a writer," I said.

"What do you write, screenplays?"

"No."

"What, then?"

"Nothing."

Alix cut in and rescued me.

"What's that guy's name," I said.

"That's Chaz. His housemate is exes with Lara."

"Who's Lara."

"Lara, the photographer?" she said, like I should know. Alix pointed her out across the room. Lara was the one with the hair the color of a ripe blood orange. The man I saw her talking with had a tight little body and wore his hair in braided pigtails. We found Sasha in the crowd. I started to taste the sour chemical paste dripping down the back of my throat so I took the glass of bourbon out of Sasha's hand, drank, put it back in his hand.

"Lovely," he said. "Here, let me introduce you to André."

"You've got great eyebrows," André said and grabbed my hand, not to shake it but to hold it.

"See?" Sasha said directly into my ear.

"I get that a lot," I said.

"Everyone who ever comes in here is on the brink of something big," he said. "This is a no-nobody zone. So, who are you?" He was wearing white leather high-top sneakers made to look dirty fresh out of the box. The drab egg the golden goose laid. I was silent.

"You don't smile much, do you?"

"Won't get crow's feet that way," I said.

I had said too much.

"I'm going to get a drink."

I was feeling even more disdainful than usual. I'd borrowed my favorite of Alix's kimonos, black itajime-dyed raw silk, left open over a white ribbed tank top and the same denim shorts I'd been wearing since I'd arrived. The air was balmy and crisp in the hills. Right away I sensed there was an ambient importance to my being seen and heard here and, certain I was going to blow it, every fiber of my being tensed up.

Darting my gaze amongst the crowd, shifting my weight and fidgeting with my clothes, I picked out other micro groups of friends, taking selfies, photographing and videoing one another with their phones. I wondered why Alix wasn't taking friendship-solidifying photos with me. Perhaps she was above such trite behavior, I thought. But that couldn't have been it, because online I'd seen photos of her with other friends, the relatively famous ones. Now those were images of people thriving. Sunning themselves on vacation together on some paradisiacal ancient Grecian beach. I reflected, impassively, in a moment of coke-induced ego reflux, that rich people got to play at life on an advanced level, and I could be good at it, too. I'd been invited, after all, into this parallel universe, but still I didn't seem to be breathing the same air.

I was introduced to a singer with hair long enough to cover her breasts, a gradient of dirty-blonde she could not plausibly have been born with—a '60s California dream personified. We struck up a conversation about her latest tour, which had taken her to Europe, the land where people kiss faces in greeting. She demonstrated on my face. "Sometimes, they kiss you two times, like this." Then she'd repeat the action. "Then some places, they give you three. Like this." She eyed me like a goshawk and drew me closer. I thought we were going to make out. Then Sasha came up to offer us each a line. She giggled, and we both snorted a line off his forearm.

The music was cut. A rather large woman started calling out for quiet in the middle of the party. She could've been 6'7" in heels. Her shoulders were far broader than her hips, and her hips were broader than my shoulders.

"I wanna start by thanking everybody for coming out," she said. "We all know why we're here."

We were, apparently, volunteer extras in a film André was making. I looked at Sasha; he shrugged, shook his head, body language indicating I was supposed to believe he hadn't known what was going on.

I got very *Truman Show*-paranoid and didn't feel comfortable being among so many people anymore.

Suddenly everyone around looked so posed, trying unnaturally hard to act natural. I wanted to go home, where I could be alone, and talk with myself by writing my stream of consciousness as fast as my hands could manifest it.

A small camera crew had set itself up while we'd all been drinking and smoking and chatting amongst ourselves. Now they asked us to dance in silence while two actors exchanged dialogue in front of the camera. The person directing went around and asked partygoers to stand in new spots so that they could fill in the shot, make it look like the actors were really in the middle of a happening party. People started smiling artificial smiles and having pretend conversations by moving their lips and emoting way more than they had before the cameras started rolling.

I insisted to Sasha and Alix that we leave at once. I stood around awkwardly while he took his sweet time saying goodbye to people. Alix was over it, too, so we went out to the car and smoked while we waited.

"I'd ask if you had fun," she smirked, "but I know you better than that."

"Thanks," I said, "at least that makes one of us."

Sasha finally stammered out of the house. "Let's go to In-N-Out," he said, reverberating with coked-out intensity, "I need to eat like an animal someplace nobody will judge me. Haha!" He thrusted his keys towards us. "You drive."

"Not it!" Alix said. We all got in. I got into the drivers seat.

I put the key in the ignition.

At the In-N-Out on Sunset Boulevard, Sasha and Alix and I were idling in the drive-thru line. We all did bumps. Then I asked Alix to switch with me and take the wheel. I didn't get back into the car. She yelled at me from the driver's seat, "Where the fuck are you going, girl? Get back in the car!"

I said "I'll see you at home," and began to walk down Sunset.

"It's 3 in the morning, you're gonna get jumped!" she yelled, but I waved and kept walking, passing a man sleeping on a bed of stuffed trash bags.

I had cigarettes, but a few blocks too late, I realized I didn't have a light. I walked to a bodega but it was closed. "Fucking hell!" I said. A young woman was walking by pushing a shopping cart that held a white garbage bag stuffed with clothing.

"Need a light?" she said, and I said, "God, yes." I offered her one of my American Spirits and she lit us both up.

"Want to go for a walk?" she said.

"It's cold." I said, "Sure."

Her name was Mariana. She'd lived in LA all her life. "Hollywood used to be much worse," she said. "I grew up in Venice Beach but I've been in this part of town for years now. It was cheaper living then, not like now."

"Where are you living now?"

"I'm kind of between places right now. I was crashing on couches and trying to find a job. Then I was sleeping in my car. Then my car got impounded and I couldn't afford to pay the fine to get it back."

"Oh."

"Yeah. I got a tent now. I just had to move it over here from downtown. There was another girl in a tent near mine. She had a baby and everything. The father was out of the picture, obviously. Then one night I was trying to sleep and I heard a commotion. Some fucking guy had gone into her tent and was raping her. She was screaming and then stopped suddenly—that's how I knew there was trouble. I abandoned the tent and left."

"You didn't help her?!"

"Nobody was there to help *me*," she said, and I understood.

"Have you ever gone to one of those shelters?"

"Yeah, once. I lived in some affordable housing, supposed to help transition people back into society and all that. But the place was infested with bedbugs, and it got so bad we all had to leave. I went to a women's shelter on Skid Row after that, but it was too full. There were all these old ladies ahead of me waiting every time I tried to get a bed. I'm still young, so I figured it was best I just take care of myself."

"God, that sounds… awful."

"Yeah, but you know, life goes on. We can adapt to anything."

We approached a tent on the edge of a carpark.

"This is me," she said. "Can I show you something?"

"Sure."

She opened her tent and gestured for me to enter. I bent over and peeked inside. There were drawings and paintings stuck up on the walls of the tent. She was an artist. She wasn't half bad.

"These are great," I said. I couldn't speak for a moment. "Sorry. I think I have to go home now."

"Oh, shit! I thought you were homeless too!"

"No, sorry," I said, and used my iPhone to call a car to come get me.

"Can you at least give me some money?" she said.

"Sure, of course, sorry—"

"Don't be sorry," she said, and I handed her five bucks.

"Thanks. God bless."

She zippered herself inside her tent. I stood on the curb waiting for my ride.

I returned to the house. I unlocked the door, locked it behind me, undressed, went to bed. But I didn't feel at home. Nothing belonged to me. No longer could I take my privilege for granted.

Here I was in California, living the real American dream: endless sunshine and leisure, counting time by my own cadence, like how the tempo of the same song differs depending on who plays it.

Variations, in musicology, are repetitions of a sequence that are slightly modified with each recitation. Repetition is powerful, but only for a spell. What gives meaning to a repetitious set is the moment of its conclusion. The sound of the end of one repetition is silence, and a beat of silence gives no measure by which to keep time. However brief, that silence can feel excruciatingly long. To be caught in one pattern is to be isolated from any experience outside of it. Repetition facilitates an illusion of normalcy. Once the silence falls, like the deafening smack of metal on metal, the shock is at first disorienting; but soon, inexplicably, that silence is clarity itself.

It had been a week since Alix had gone to London and I had not spoken to another person. Loneliness cast over that beautiful house on that beautiful land in the Canyon. The holding pattern discontinued, and life became strange again. Alix's presence had given me permission to feel I belonged here. Now I was an aimless tourist. I reflected that I felt very much the same as I had felt in New York—that I did not belong here nor there—but here, at least, I was not so stressed out. At least I had some peace and quiet.

I wrapped my naked body in one of Alix's vintage silk kimonos and descended to the patio, barefoot on dead grass and earth. A coyote came gamboling out from the brush with a rabbit squirming in its mouth. The coyote and I held eye contact for a moment in total stillness. The rabbit flinched in the clench of his jaw. The coyote jerked his head back, straightened up, and bounded off, stage right, through the trees.

I hid inside, reverberating nervous energy, unable to think. At some point along those long, lonesome days, the distinction between outdoors and indoors ceased to exist, or no longer mattered. There was no air conditioning in that old house, and the windows weren't shaped right to install one. I managed to keep myself busy throughout the mornings, but come three in the afternoon I grew resentful of my lack of company. To take the edge off, I'd go for long walks through the Canyon. The exercise and fresh air alleviated a bit of the anxiety that would otherwise render me a trembling husk of myself. By the time the gloom had burnt away under the oppressive sunlight, I'd get home, shower, and eat. My preferred pastime was to select a book that came with the house, lie in the hammock, and read until the sun went down.

One afternoon I was reading Joan Didion and taking notes. "Some Dreamers of the Golden Dream," April 1966, the story of a San Bernardino woman who was convicted of burning her husband to death: "The future always looks good in the golden land, because no one remembers the past."

I too wished to forget I had ever lived any other life. So I went online and deleted all of my social media accounts. I hadn't checked anything since I'd come to California anyway. The last thing my fragile ego needed was a confirmation of my suspicion that nobody missed me. I thought of her famous aphorism, "We tell ourselves stories in order to live," until I had deconstructed it down to its marrow: people have an inexplicable urge to articulate their every lived experience into narrative. We may take stories and storytelling for granted, but it is necessary for our mental and emotional stability, especially concerning random cruelties: those experiences that defy language or logic, those traumas, sudden deaths, freak accidents, and states of shock. These instances are what make the "in order to live" part of the phrase important; we must reduce the confusion, horror, and chaos of the universe by narrativizing our experience at the micro and macro levels. We need to make sense of everything, even if that means leaning into the nonsensical nature of things when the words come too slowly, when language fails to reassure us.

The world's libraries and museums contain at least eighteen books whose bindings have been identified as human skin. It's called anthropodermic bibliopegy. I want what I write to be a literal piece of me. Not a growth or spawn, but a sacrificial, binding, purposeful severance of some undesirable part of myself. If I could figure out where the lazy and afraid and bad in me lives, I would cut it out and turn it into something useful.

I had been counting time by the sounding wind chime. When the wind was still I couldn't still my mind. I walked down to the Country Store, exchanged glances with babes in fringed suede jackets dipping their manicured, bony hands into their designer handbags for cash, picking up their packs of American Spirits, picking indifferently at their salads in the shade on the old wooden patio. The walk home from the Country Store up the main road that wound up into the Canyon was my daily exercise when I didn't feel up for a hike. Images congealed into prose as I walked, and then I sat cross-legged outside of the cabin, typing dutifully, the stenographer of my stream of consciousness. Sheltered by hills and old-growth wood and the mythopoesis of Laurel Canyon, nothing I wrote down seemed to be of much consequence.

There was an old sound system in the house. After wiping out my social media presence, I went inside and put on the first record I saw: Handel's aria, "Saeviat Tellus Inter Rigores." The sun was setting behind the rising peaks and treetops that framed the sky over the Canyon. I caught my reflection in a mirror on the wall and locked eyes with it, at first not recognizing myself. There was a beauty mark just above my cheekbone to the left of my left eye. It was reversed in the mirror image; I felt for it on the wrong side. It was the defining indicator of selfhood on the left side of my face, the side I preferred in my self-image delusion of symmetry, a right brain/ left brain thing, or so I had read. I hit the Chihuly bong one more time and scrutinized the mole up close. The grotesque little thing had been the *coup-de-cœur* of my ex. It punctuated the way I was seen, brought curiosity to an abrupt end, designated a final judgment of who I was based on something so arbitrary as the cosmic roll of the genetic dice.

On my forehead, just below the hairline, was something I hadn't noticed before. A little red blood bubble—a cherry angioma, a sign of aging. It was grotesque and wiggly and delicate and I wanted it gone. I rifled through the bathroom drawers for the nail-trimming scissors. I pulled the skin taut, held the sharp edge close as possible to where the little red blood-bubble rose out of the skin, and snipped. It didn't hurt as much as the slicing sensation made me cringe. I felt lightheaded, then enthralled, then horrified. I sat on the front porch with a bottle of alcohol and a bag of cotton balls, applying pressure, waiting on my body to forgive me and for the tiny gushing wound to coagulate. When I thought the bleeding must have stopped and discarded the cotton ball, blood again began to flow down the side of my face. I went digging through the drawers in the kitchen. I found a shucking knife and a lighter. I held the flame to the knife's tip to get it hot. I looked in the mirror again. My breasts stiffened—with nightfall had come the chilled desert air. I pressed the hot tip of the knife to the spot where the angioma had been, cauterizing the wound.

The aria ended, but the record kept turning. The *blip!...*
blip! slowed the silence with agonizing precision.

I hate those dismal doctor's office waiting rooms, with fluorescent lighting and sickly white grid-panelled ceilings with blackened puckering like stale cheese-cloth—likely cradling the microscopic rot of every other body that's passed into that room before. Each plastic support beam holds every ceiling tile in place, caked on the inside with generations of dead insects and dust. The smell betrays the filth that, while kept politely out of sight, looms just overhead. As above, so below: I wretch at wall-to-wall carpeting. Linoleum nauseates me. So many hideous buildings built on shoestring budgets designated for the lowest common denominator of society: people in need. Such offensive and unfor-tunate design is the detritus of decades-old unattended collisions between bad taste and cheapskate investment, the brainchild of those regrettably hasty adopters of bad new trends, of some real estate developer's neglectful flinging of permanent solutions at the needs of the human environment. Vinyl siding, popcorn ceilings, synthetic berber carpet, particle board. The eeriness of replicas applies even to the most banal commodities. There in that waiting room, an early childhood resentment came rushing back to the fore of my mind: my repulsion at the ugliness that comes with being less fortunate.

I had come to the mental health clinic to get a prescription for antidepressants. I got the idea when I read that Nick Drake had killed himself by swallowing thirty Amitriptyline pills.

I knew something was wrong with my head because I could no longer focus long enough to read an entire page. Meaning ceased to mean anything at all, or I no longer cared to make sensible connections. In attempts to clear this haze of writer's block, I tried to write, but what came out was badly pastiched fragments and non-sequitous phrases.

Psychophysiology of analysis of connotative decodification:
Very bad; too bad to be ignored.

Psychedelics and the acute confusional state.

The etiology of my alexithymia: a comorbid dysfunction of sensing and caring.

Pathology of fugue. Where A: a musical composition in which one or two themes are repeated or imitated by successively entering voices and contrapuntally developed in a continuous interweaving of the voice parts, and B: a disturbed state of consciousness in which one seems to perform acts in full awareness but, upon recovery, cannot recollect the acts performed... I am not A, but B.

Sitting in that waiting room, anticipating another's skewed analysis of my problem, it occurred to me that perhaps I had always failed at pretending not to be insane. Resistance to my insanity had, perhaps, only exacerbated it. Everything bad I'd ever done could've been a subconscious knee-jerk reaction to my attempts at assimilation into a society where I simply didn't belong. Writing was the only time I felt right, for I wanted nothing more than to have myself figured out, but I also believed and knew that nobody wanted to listen to me wringing my mind in my hands.

I was led into a room with makeshift particle board walls and left alone to sit in a stained-upholstery chair while I waited for a social worker to make a treatment plan with me. I could hear the session happening in the adjoining room through the flimsy wall. I imagined, based on the voice, a middle-aged white man, an obstinately stoic, working-class family man with a temper. The therapist had a softer, younger male voice.

The patient sounded stern but the words got caught a little in his throat on the way out like he was about to cry. "I work hard, I bust my ass, but it never seems to amount to anything. I've supported a family for almost twenty years and we've never progressed past the point of struggling from paycheck to paycheck. I'm just so tired all the time. I love my family, but sometimes I wonder what the point is."

I thought of my father, who could and would have said the same thing, but I couldn't imagine him going to therapy, which he'd disparaged as self-indulgence for those with nothing better to do. It'd been awhile since the image of my father had shown up in my mind. I realized I also hadn't thought much about what Marcel was going through, having returned home and found me gone. Perhaps I'd left the symbolic order of phallic signification. On the other side of the wall, the softer voice replied some validating truism too low for me to make out.

Like any reverent feminist I had demonized the patriarchy, disparaged it openly. It felt good against the frailty of my ego. In practice, I had shamelessly, repeatedly prostrated myself before it. The cities I'd set myself up in, the clothes I'd put on my body, the "work" I'd occupied myself with, the friends I'd camouflaged myself with, the college education I'd mantled myself with, the obsessive grooming, the plucking, the waxing, the shaving, the cleansing, the exfoliating, everything in the name of pleasing the men so that the men would provide a comfortable life for me. Self-care was invisible labor even I didn't perceive as particularly useful or meaningful. I'd flailed through every effort at ladylike self-discipline and restraint. I lived in devotion or martyrdom to an idealized, man-pleasing vision of my would-be/could-be self. A ritualistic cycle of self-destruction, a series of little acts of violence motivated by self-loathing. I was broke. I was an impostor, not a real writer. I had stolen from my last boyfriend and abandoned him. I was untrustworthy, unstable, and unlovable. My only route to salvation was to lie to myself about all of this convincingly enough to make the lies sound like truth to anyone else.

The social worker entered, shut the door behind her, sat down behind her fake-wood desk, and began by asking me about my current substance use, about my childhood.

The drugs, and the drinking, they are called self-destruction but—in truth—they are tools of *decon*struction. Substance abuse is the ultimate means of delayed decoding. Our instincts demand we reset the humanity construct, make us into beasts fighting in vain against a need to be our disgusting selves. Vices are not destruction of the self; vices are destruction of the mask that's soldered on from infancy. Of course the underneath is ugly; it's been denied daylight all our lives. It's all pulp and atrophy under there—my god, the stench! The humanimal self is all that we are taught to hate. We would not know what to do with it if we all agreed to access it. But it is only so loathsome because we've never let it form. Without the lie of humanity, we are the liquid state between caterpillar and butterfly.

All of it, far too much, occurred to me in a slew of emotion that had me sobbing, nose running, before I'd even answered all of her rudimentary psych-eval questions. When it was over, she sent me to reception to make a follow-up appointment, but I just left.

The opacity of the universe was thinning. Nothing meant anything but to make something of nothing. I had been drawn out west in the first place because I was unsatisfied living in creative stasis under the impression that only hard reality could turn a profit. Everything needed to make less sense or I was going to lose it completely. I'd been raised poor and without any spiritual practice, but my parents had at least raised me to think for myself. They had always encouraged me to draw and write and sing and dance, and in the initial years of adulthood I had become joyless without any grounding practice to accompany myself through times of solitude. Concrete brain, results-based projections of time-use value. I had all the words, but what was the point? I kept writing the same love letter over and again in the ink of an afterthought.

> *Cymatics: modal phenomena: visible sound co-vibration imprinting on a membrane the modes of vibration, the oscillation of my organ of vision, my circadian adjustments: parabolic superposition.*

> *It's just such an imposition. So? Fuck me in the vitreous, lover, fuck me in the afternoon, in the gelatinous mass of my brittle star, in my water salt sugar collagen, baby, right in my temporal range! Are we deforesting or preserving the phytogeography of my pubis while you're shuffling your hips to scooch beneath my hubris?*

> *"Did you come?" Why do you ask me when you could feel for it? Can't you be satisfied by an off-screen climax if the suggestion holds? Can't you read the vibrations in the purging of my clear-warm-everything?*

I was amorous in adjacent dimensions. I was suffering a hysterical pregnancy: not a maternal delusion, but as if my belly was host to a rift in space-time. My body was rejecting my brain as if it was a transplanted organ. I was all alone in a post-metamodern void of malformed hack-think, penning depravity psalms and anaphoric aphorisms. I was so far gone I didn't have language for where I was. I had literally succumbed to nothing, backed myself into a corner, clawed out of artifice and found myself in unrecognisable environs, naked as a spermatozoa, and nestled in yet another farce of a life.

I couldn't sleep. Around three or four in the morning I couldn't take the stillness anymore, so I got into the car. I opened all of the compartments and found a CD, an audiobook called *Letting Go*. I put it on and drove aimlessly. The narrator explained that we can simply let go of our feelings, but that we usually employ more self-destructive methods: suppression, repression, expression, escape. I turned onto a westbound highway. "Escape is the avoidance of feelings through diversion," said the voice filling the empty cabin of the Prius.

I realized I hadn't yet been to Big Sur, so I made for the Pacific Coast Highway and headed north into the verdant coastland. There were still barely any other cars on the road as the sun peeked over the wooded mountains to the east. The hopefulness of the audiobook offended my hopeless sensibility, so I turned it off and put my music on shuffle instead. A rough demo recording of Jason Molina came on. I could hear in his voice all the years of suffering behind the words "long, dark blues..." Perhaps life was too long, and he'd divined the futility of the exercise, yet he mustered the will to sing and play his guitar to keep life going as long as he could.

Deep inside my chest, I felt a swelling sensation, like liquid under pressure. I turned the music off. I decided that once I came to the highest point of those majestic cliffs, I would drive off the edge.

I had been driving in silence for a few hours, shifting focus rapidly between the views and the road, waiting for the most imposing height to reveal itself to me, when the road disappeared into the forest. Out of sight of the Pacific Ocean and the gorgeous edge of the continent, I feared I had missed my chance. It was impossible to turn the car around, and I didn't know where the road would come out. Then I saw a sign for the Henry Miller Library. I was distracted looking at it when something large and living materialized upon the hood of the car.

I swerved onto the sandy shoulder, narrowly avoided hitting a tree. The windshield had a crack in it, but I was alright. I got out and kneeled down beside the deer. A beat-down pickup truck approached and pulled over. The man got out and promptly put a bullet through her head. Even in California, we're still in America, I thought.

"I'll take it if you won't," he said.

"By all means," I said.

To my horror, the Prius wouldn't start. While I called the roadside assistance number on the insurance papers in the glove compartment, the man wrapped the dead deer in a tarp and loaded it onto the flatbed of his truck.

"Where d'ya live?"

"LA," I said.

"What part? Big town."

"Laurel Canyon."

"Come again?"

"It's, like, Hollywood."

"Well, I'm headed for San Diego. Hollywood isn't exactly on the way. But I'll give y'a ride."

Delirious, I left the keys in the car, left it unlocked, and got into his truck.

It was a long, uncomfortable silence. Finally we pulled up to the house. The man slowly eased the vehicle around back through grass and brush, parked, struggled with the weight of the carcass, got it to the sturdiest-looking of the seven trees, tossed a line over the best lowest branch, strung the thing up, leaned it against an adjacent stump that had once been used to split firewood. I brought him a glass of water. "You got any money, I'll sort it out for you," he said. I said I didn't. "Well then!" he said, lighting a cigarette, "you're on your own, missy." And he got in his truck and drove away.

I sat still on the ground before the hanging carcass a while. I looked at my feet, now bare. I articulated my toes and watched the thin phalanges, bones and blue blood veins move against my skin. I was meditating, I suppose, to come to terms with the sanctity of my insides. I knew what to do, having witnessed my father disassemble several of the delicate beasts. I knew to twist and pop a joint apart. I knew to apply significant pressure when I made a cut because hesitation makes waste. I knew to follow the fibrous guidelines. I knew to cut with, not against, the grain.

Hesitation is the surest sign of a conscientious nature—or, at the very least, self-consciousness of one's weakness. To act impulsively, instinctually, is to be most in-tune with nature. Not that to be in tune with nature is some sublime ideal. Tidal waves do not hesitate to crash on a coastal city. Animals do not hesitate to attack or react if instinct demands it. If storms are "acts of god," as the government or insurance companies are fond of calling them, god is inextricable from physical nature and has no humanity.

The sun inched across the sky. The shade of the tree where the deer was hanging wouldn't last much longer. Rigor mortis had begun to set in; its legs were sticking up stiff.

I cut through the hide right above the sternum on the chest plate. I made the first opening and got the blade underneath the hide, lifted the hide with two fingers as I cut through it, trying to avoid puncturing anything, though as I navigated the body I didn't know what organ was what. I had cut about six to eight inches into it, over the breastplate from sternum to its bloated belly. When I cut into the body cavity, all the pressure that had built up from the internal bleeding made a whoosh sound like a tire that had a nail puncture in it, hissing quietly as the gases escaped. I stepped back from the putrid metallic odor. No stopping now or the whole thing would go to waste, I thought. I got back up close to the opening of the body cavity. A swarm of flies coated the carcass. I still had to paunch it before I could separate the meat.

Then the hornets swarmed around. I tried to brush them off but they were relentless, trying to burrow into the body cavity. They ignored me entirely, didn't sting me once. I kept cutting, pulled back the skin, reached my arms in and started pulling at the connective tissues, reached in right up to my shoulders to free the intestines and stomach from the rib cage. I went up to the throat, cut through its esophagus and windpipe to the bone. I reached back into the chest cavity, found the tubes, and cut them free, still shooing the hornets away. I had a garbage bag sitting at the ass-end of the deer. I grabbed the internal organs and rolled them out of the deer and into the garbage bag in one motion. I cut the final bit of the intestines out and got the remnants into the bag. The hornets and flies were clinging to me and the deer. The shade was receding quickly. In desperation, I took the garden hose and sprayed the carcass down, which drove the hornets off. I grabbed the knife and started skinning the deer, sliding the blade horizontally under the hide. Not a minute later, the hornets were back.

I went into the storage shed around the side of the house and found a pail with a handle on it. I used the pail handle to steady the head of the hose and turned it on, and it sprayed upwards, showering a mist over the carcass. The swarm of hornets dissipated. I stood over the animal and under the spray, the water so cold it shocked my lungs, shortened my breath. I took up the knife and got back in there, got enough of the skin off to get to the meat.

I stepped out of the hose-rain and marvelled at the surreality of the scene. I was reminded of San Bartolomeo Scorticato, the flayed apostle I'd seen illustrated in one of the old books in the house.

I started hacking through the meat. I threw the meat into the hose pail. Peeled back more skin, cut away more meat. Time ceased to pass. I put the garbage bag of blood, bones, and fur into the city-sanctioned can and sprayed everything down with the hose. I cleaned and packed the meat into freezer bags to store for later. The animal had probably saved my life, and now I could eat like a red-blooded queen for months.

Time just kept on standing still around me. I knew that to other people time seemed to be moving constantly, but alone, time seemed to be in abundance, undermining every capitalistic notion I'd ever had of squandering mine. Money, too, had always meant too much to me, but now it had stopped meaning anything except survival and freedom. My having or having-not had a certain luxurious existence never defined me, really. This privilege was bound to expire, was too good to be true, I should've known better. I'd abandoned the life I'd been building with a willing partner, all to chase a vain shortcut to a level of success I hadn't earned. But it was already done, and I thought I might as well enjoy it while it lasted.

I was lying on my back, looking up at the sun through the old growth trees that slouched over the yard, puffing on a joint. I was thinking back on the lysergic bliss of my first time tripping with Alix. I longed for more: more time away on a new kind of vacation in the pre-memory, pre-trauma wilderness of the conscious psyche, unadulterated by the word *no*. The Lacanian *nom du père* is a machete marking trees to stake out the boundaries of consciousness. The ego is an electric fence charged by fear. For a moment, I felt how it had felt the last time I had been on acid, when hours slipped by like a soothing breeze and the air felt like bathing in velvet. I flipped through a copy of *Be Here Now* by Ram Dass. How I envied the Maharaj-ji's power to exist in the primary state of consciousness at all times. There, at last, was the meaningful pursuit worth living for.

Then Alix called me. "Can we meet up tomorrow?"

"Of course." But, for the first time, I dreaded seeing her.

I made my way soberly into the day-world.

A little girl in heart-shaped pastel-plastic sunglasses cooed and smiled at a man, whom I presumed to be her father, sitting at a table in the café where Alix and I had agreed to meet. The man, with his head in his hand, smiled at the little girl. The pretty young woman in the red coat waiting in line looked at the little girl with her father at the table, lowered her eyes and smiled. I looked at the pretty young woman and she looked back at me. The pretty young woman looked at the little girl and her father, then looked at me again, and smiled. Her look was knowing. Her knowingness irked me. Finally—like, in an instant, but after what felt to me an epoch—I relented and smiled back to defuse tension. This hostile exchange became common once I had reached adulthood, be it from relatives, strangers, or annoying acquaintances: a presumptuous bet against me continuing as I was, betraying their true judgmental presuppositions that a woman of my age with no ring on her finger and no child at her teat must be unfulfilled. Isn't this divine, and that will be you someday, just you wait, it will happen, time makes fools of us all and then we die. The audacity of their winking smiles.

I was in a terrible, misanthropic mood. I accidentally made eye contact with a slender, serious young woman eating a cupcake. She looked up at me with ferocious eyes, like if she could tell I was judging her she'd lose her shit. I took my coffee and sat at a table outside instead. I'd quit smoking months ago but today was a special occasion, so I took out a pack of American Spirits and lit one. Just then, Alix approached, looking positively glamorous in cat-eye sunglasses and an expensive-looking black leather tote bag slung over her shoulder. I straightened my posture and corrected for my terse mannerisms at once. I had to mentally prepare to be myself for her.

When we embraced, she inhaled deeply through her nose, then sighed with what sounded like relief.

"You smell just like you used to," she said, still hugging me. The sun on us, we sat facing one another with our cups of coffee and our hands on the table.

"What were you doing in Big Sur?" she said.

Puzzled at how to begin to answer, I blurted it out.

"Well, I was planning on killing myself."

"I can't fucking believe you," she said.

"What?" I assumed she meant totaling the car.

She gave me a look I'd never seen her face make before. I apologized and asked what it would take for her to forgive me. Could she just let me have it? Unload everything she'd never told me for fear of hurting my feelings? As expected, she declined, but I insisted: she'd actually be doing me a favor, and I wanted to earn her trust back somehow. I was gripped with fear that she'd kick me out and never speak to me again.

"I'm worried about you," she said, grasping my hands over the table.

I scrutinized her face for pity but found none. I averted her gaze, too ashamed to look her in the eyes. She'd always believed in me more than I'd ever believed in myself and I let her down. The surrounding noise ceased to register; all I could hear was the soft power of all the small mechanisms of the universe, as loud as someone screaming in my ears.

"You've given me a chance here, a chance to come and start something totally new, to live and thrive—I've had shelter, time, support, and I've squandered it. You welcomed me here and I am grateful. I feel like a failure. I want to be better."

"You are not a failure. If you were a failure we'd have nothing to talk about. You're just going through a rough patch. I'm concerned, but I believe in you. It's not as if you're even in any real trouble."

"Seriously? I'm a mess. I'm broke, I wrecked your car, and I have nothing of value to offer the world."

"Calla, don't be ridiculous. This city's whole mythology was built on people so fucked up they could barely fit in with society, but somehow, here, they thrived. Not that I'm anyone to judge. You just have to decide what your priorities are and fill your time, just like everyone else."

"I guess I should go back to work."

"Whatever you do, just do me a favor and get your shit together," she smiled. She rose from her seat, as did I, and drew me in for a hug and said, "I love you."

"I'm not worthy," I answered.

"Are you mad about the Prius?"

She sighed. "No, I'm not mad about the Prius. I'm mad you wanted to kill yourself."

"I won't do it again," I said.

"You'd better fucking not." The repairs to the car had been covered, she explained, because she had added me as an additional driver to her insurance. And I could have it back, as long as I promised not to drive it off a cliff.

I promised.

I used a rideshare app to get myself a ride home. A young woman picked me up in a Honda Civic. She mentioned she'd lived in the area since she was born. I said, wow, you must have seen a lot of changes. She said it really wasn't that bad, at least there's less crime now, but the old culture is gone, the old businesses are gone, all the people of the neighborhood who all used to know each other and run their community here are gone. There used to be regular shootings right there, and now there's a farmer's market. Some of the same old people are still here, though, you see them now and then. They've always been here. They're still around.

"I've never felt that connected to a place in my life," I said. She laughed, but I hadn't meant to be funny.

Back in the house, the weight of that encounter with Alix settled in. I was overcome by a relentless, throbbing pressure in my head that shot little lightning-bolts of pain into my neck, and I tensed up my shoulders and back, as if my body was bracing itself for some impact. Darkness has a way of clinging to the withdrawn, to close spaces and narrow intentions, to perforations opening onto unlit insides.

I got high, undressed, and lay naked in the backyard. The only sound was the cacophony of birdsong ricocheting from a cluster of trees. Alix had mentioned that many a pet parrot had escaped its owner and formed a flock, a noisy blight on the hills. They were poor fliers; that's how you could tell them apart from any other flock of bird—that, and their eerie screeching that ricocheted throughout the Canyon. What kind of cretin would keep one, I wondered.

I spaced out for I couldn't say how long, each moment excruciatingly slow. I noticed my breasts, my soft belly, my bush, the faded stretch marks on the insides of my thighs, the fleshy peach glow of the sky. I had no plans, no desire but to lay still, but I was restless, compulsively searching my body for flaws to scrutinize. A nervous tick. I self-medicated with more cannabis, lulled myself into a false sense of security with no contingency plan.

The next day Alix got the car back from the shop and suggested I go to Joshua Tree.

"I think the desert will do you good," she said.

In the Prius I packed a gallon jug of water, a ruled notebook and a pen, a small baggie with four tabs of LSD, my ID, and my phone. Inching along in traffic on the way out of the interminable city sprawl, my death drive overpowered everything. I wanted to wake all the way up, or else sleep forever.

I drove through miles of dry sands and hills and wind-mills and gas stations and fast food chains, past the road signs advertising Palm Springs, through the Canyon and the Yucca Valley, where I turned off onto the road cutting through Joshua Tree National Park. Campsites sprawled out with their designated fire pits and picnic tables, families and frat boys pitching tents side by side on patches of turf drawn in the cleared brush: our side, your side. I kept on until all signs of civilization had thinned out to a sublime quiet. The sky was a glowy fresco of orange and pink; it reminded me of the store-brand sherbet my mother bought on hot summer days when I was a kid. The trees looked Seussian with their tufted limbs, stuck out against the wide-open expanse of burnt sienna, crowded with brambly brush, senna bushes, saguaro and cholla cacti. I kept driving deeper into the void, yearning to be beyond help. I stopped only once I felt lost enough to swerve off-road, unseen. I walked away from the car in the direction of the sunset and placed the tabs of acid on my tongue one at a time. I watched the light being vacuumed off the desert floor and into the horizon. Emotionally flatlining, supernaturally indifferent. Soon, the fear. Alone in the vast, hostile desert, bracing for the chemicals to override my cerebral norm, I watched the earth turn over into total darkness.

The crest of the big wave broke, euphoria washed over me, all was right with the world. The thought occurred suddenly that I had to make amends with Marcel. To look at my phone's screen nauseated me; the pixels vibrated and danced around on the screen, the colorful icons distorted. The last remnants of light broke over the crests of the distant silhouetted mountains, dusting the spiky tufts at the ends of the Joshua trees' arms. The signal was weak. I walked around in crude circles with my arm extended to the sky, hoping to make contact. To my surprise, I found a spot with just enough reception, and I called him. When he answered, "Calla?" I immediately regretted the decision.

"Calla? Where are you?!"

"Joshua Tree," I said. "I took too much acid and now I can't find my car."

He sighed without relief.

"When are you coming back?"

I could hear him breathing progressively heavier the longer I sustained my silence.
"I'm sorry," I said.

"Weren't we happy together?" he said through what sounded like tears.

"You were my only happiness," I said.

"You can still come back," he said. "Come home."

"I'm sorry," I repeated, uselessly. "I don't deserve you."

He kept talking, but my hands felt like they were dissolving, my fingers withering, and I dropped the phone. I began to hyperventilate. I knew I was crying, but my body had gone almost completely numb, all sensation replaced with a sharp tingling or else no sensation at all. I began to exhale pained vowels with every sob, *oh... ha...* like an inconsolable child.

I felt crowded by the burnt-orange rock formations, plutons and batholiths, who I noticed now to be living, leviathan lichen, and I walked in the direction of the disappearing shadows until my third eye no longer recognized me.

The moon was full and uncomfortably close, passing over the desert at a dizzying speed like a floodlight hanging from a drone. The thing had eyes, I was certain, and teeth, with which it gnawed its way across the sky. The grim moonlight illuminated a four-dimensional grid in the atmosphere. Refractions moved pixelated against the expanse of nothing. I watched the horizon bleed out as the air grew colder. The sand was swallowing and birthing in kaleidoscope shapes. I got up close to it, observed the spindly roots like ancient fingers reaching out from the grave. That rattlesnake off in the brush wanted to run me up its spine-tree. The messiah trees naked and aflame. The creature in the sky breathed down my neck. Breathed fire on my back. Breathed fire on my little breasts. My skin peeled off in sheets like the old wallpaper in my great-grandmother's house after she died. I counted time by the skin I lost. On my forearms and hands was a film of spider's silk. The creature in the sky was the genesis of object permanence when he slipped out of sight breathing heavy and low under my feet. I fell onto my palms and resigned myself to the earth, face-down, stinging. Something's got my ankle. Something's raising my leg by the ankle, pressing down on the nape of my neck, as if to drown me in the sand.

The drought was not a drought, but the desert eating the greener land. The leviathan spirit Mojave, wide awake, stretched its tanned hide all the way to the Pacific Ocean, hooking itself on the crags of Big Sur like canvas on a splintered wood frame. Elation came, then laughter, then a complete release of fear. Not a delusion of universal benevolence but fearless amusement with the absurdity of it all.

I'd poured myself out through the sand sieve of the desert floor, filtered toxicities and bad habits like gold from the filament. I walked around in circles delighted and rubbing my palm on the peach-fuzz brush that grew close to the ground. The brush appeared, in my altered state of lysergic wonderment, to be disconnected from the ground it grew out of, just like I could not fathom my own mind-body tether. I walked barefoot over snake holes as if the rosy boas and sundried rattlers were but myth or mirage.

The Ideal-I went translucent in the floodlight of the full moon, lighting up the silhouette of my inner child, and we writhed together on the parched ground to the cries of baby coyotes nearby. I shivered, having come unprepared for the drastic temperature drop of a desert nightfall. I felt the static electricity where my skin meets the matrix of space and time. I paced the throughlines, the Xs and Ys. I got lost in the meridian where I end and the rest begins. I climbed atop a gargantuan boulder and declared it my safe space. The hostile desert was a place of play, the wise ancient eagle-head boulders my chutes and ladders, the horizon a holographic wallpaper. Nothing could hurt me. Everything could have hurt me, but it didn't.

The edges of the horizon began to glow. From the vantage point atop the boulder, the desert floor appeared to be flooding with light. Then the sun chased the moon out of the sky.

I walked away from the sunrise until I arrived back at the road, found the car. I drove deliciously slow, swerving here and there to avoid the flashes of rainbow grid that presented themselves like a neon sign waning in opacity, until I reached Twentynine Palms. I was writhing in my skin like my skeleton wanted to burst free as the waves hit relentlessly, weakening me until I would be dragged out by the undertow of time.

I went inside, sat down at a table, requested water and a menu. I drank the entire glass of water as the server stood by; he refilled my glass. I proceeded to order a meal so abundant it seemed delightfully absurd, especially in the high desert: blueberry pancakes, bacon and soft-scrambled eggs, avocado on the side, a bowl of fresh fruit, orange juice, coffee, and a slice of cherry pie. I don't even like cherry, but couldn't resist the Lynchian symbolism in this remote diner. Paranoid that the server had given me the side-eye as he left my table, I went to the restroom and looked at myself in the mirror. I was sunburnt and coated with a film of dust; the only clean thing was my dress, because I had stripped down to nothing but my boots. I took a bath in the sink until someone pounded on the bathroom door.

Back at my table, I took an ice cube from the water glass and let it melt on the back of my neck. I ate some of everything and asked to take the pie, and another cup of coffee, to go. The server brought a box for the slice of pie and left the check on the table. I didn't have any money, but I still had Marcel's credit card. I had the server try it. It came back declined. "I must have left my other credit card in my car," I said, "let me just go get it." I went out to the car and drove back to LA.

I returned to the city a shell of myself, or, more accurately, having molted the shell of myself. Did the snakes not bite my heels in the night because they, too, had molted, and were hiding?

In the days that followed my desert trip, it seemed imperative to ease back into the civilized world, although I felt like an alien and now perceived most things to be absolutely arbitrary. As I came down, it occurred to me just how lucky I was to have avoided trouble, and that I oughtn't push my luck any further. So I decided to try to be good.

I got a job as a copywriter for a tech startup up in Silicon Valley. I found it online. Never had to leave the house—even the interviews were conducted via video call. And the pay was more than I'd ever been paid before. I can't account for this apparent stroke of luck, can't say I worked particularly hard to earn it. My capitalist's survival instinct kicked in, enabling me to sense or deduce whatever it was the boss wanted me to say. But I couldn't keep from thinking that, had the Prius not been designed such that a head-on collision with a terrestrial ungulate would incapacitate its electrical system, I would be dead, meaning I would never have to work another day in my life. For the sake of my pride, at least, I'd like to think I would've seen it through.

Besides the money, the job gave me renewed ambition: I soon realized that churning out banal line after line was a personal affront to my actual potential—which made me realize that I believed in my potential as a writer. Having a purpose in the outside world made the solitude more bearable. Already I felt more like a person, connected to the present via routine: a productive stasis I'd resisted and taken for granted all my life. Once embraced, I wrote most of the day, taking breaks to take walks or to eat, and at night I got high and listened to the sonorous cries of baby coyotes.

Winter came, and with it, the first rain I'd seen in LA. It rained that season more than Southern California had seen in five years. The arid brown hills exploded into verdancy. Throughout the state, mudslides went careening into houses and roads, even washed out the bridge up in Big Sur I'd driven across on my failed suicide mission. The parched mountainsides collapsed where not held together by robust roots. The soil depends on that which grows within it. I envied the unspoken arrangement, how it satisfies without satisfying: the structural integrity of one, the lifegiving need of the other. The roots don't ask to grow in the dirt; the dirt does not argue with the roots. The mountainside doesn't care if it is washed out. If the whole does not hold, the plants end up elsewhere, or grow differently, like the trees whose spindly tendrils stay in place where the earth has fallen away. Life goes on without complaint. I wanted to be like the the stoic trees that cling: wisely indifferent, peacefully resilient.

In the Canyon, at least, everything had held that season, or so it looked from my walks. I found comfort in the same old habits. I went out and spent money just to be around other people. I took myself out to dinners alone and tipped generously. I got acquainted with certain bartenders. Out on the little smoking patio at Café Stella, I bummed American Spirits from fashionable somebodies and eavesdropped on them as they talked shit into the warm evening air. I didn't miss the equivalent routine I'd lived in Brooklyn. I intuited something more dignified about getting drunk with a backdrop of carnal flowers and gawky, towering palms in lieu of skyscrapers.

I woke up on my 26th birthday having versed a year in a flat circle. The day passed without celebration. The air was still, hot, and dry. I called my parents to apologize for ghosting. My mother cried. I wrote Marcel a letter of apology that went on so long and so aimlessly, I abandoned the project and left it lying open on the kitchen table.

Nothing could tempt me now but a vacation to a primary state of consciousness. I found the little velvet-lined jewelry box where Alix kept her drugs.

The precise memories of that night in Joshua Tree had gone cold quickly, but the afterglow had remained. The freefall sensation of complete release from the ego's grip echoed in my very being, like a distant voice fondly calling my name. I longed for that perilous expanse of everything and nothing, hidden and venomous predators holed up waiting to receive me, barefoot on that film of peach-fuzz moss hovering over the sandy ground where the rosy boas hid. My twenty-seventh rotation around the sun seemed as good a time as any to remember that everything had always existed before me and everything will continue to exist without me, that my presence meant relatively little, that what I would leave behind would cease to mean anything—and that gave me some comfort.

I slipped one of the tabs under my tongue, then another a half-hour later. About an hour later, I became aware of the tongue, this ludicrous muscle in my head. I tongued the final tab. My lucidity was tempered only by my constitutional unease: the thought of eating, of using my tongue for anything but to talk, repulsed me, I had to face it. I wrapped myself tight in blankets, wrestled my distant body onto the hammock to the cricket songs of evening dwindling into night, and held on.

Looking out over the suicide-drop at the other precarious mountainside bungalows across the way, the glow from the windows, the occasional passing of shadows, I saw the world as it was with no meddling sense of self to cloud my vision. Egolessness affords such clarity! No fears, just observations, like I had become an invisible eyeball.

I remained like that for what felt like hours, narrating the universe as the night dragged on, getting colder. With every micromovement in my body, I felt submerged in liquid velvet, breathing it, like being back in the womb. Gravity's ripples had reached us. They were found to carry a message of collapse-as-unity, death-as-becoming: two black holes became one, and we heard the echo like a chirp from the moment of climax, a bashful orgasmic peep. The irreverence of the truth of all things. The cosmic joke, and I was in on it.

Absentmindedly shivering in the cold, I marveled at the fabric of the universe. I was in for six to twelve hours of thrashing about in what felt like a cosmic tide, waves crashing over me one after the other.

It was different this time, not least because I was in the comfort of home. The fear of death was flowing through me. I paced the house, the yard, then the house again, but the fear had overridden all memory and all future hope. The fear gripped my organs. I could feel the churning within my guts. I was narrating all of this out loud. Pacing, I stopped mid-stride, I took a knee and found my way onto the floor. I laid on my back on the hardwood and said, "I give up."

I felt something rush out of me. Like my consciousness was evacuating my body—or I'd lost the delusion that consciousness and body are separable. Breathing shallow and quick and drenched in sweat and fear, my eyes rolled back into my skull and corporeality eluded me at last.

I willed myself not to grind my molars too much while I waited for the waves to relent. I went to the bathroom and made meaningful eye contact with my gaunt face in the mirror as I brushed my teeth. I noticed the scar where the cherry angioma had been, the first tell of aging that I'd cut off impulsively. I inspected the scar closely. I stood back a bit from the mirror and looked at my naked self as if I'd never seen it before. I looked tiny, frail, pale with dark sunken-in bags under my big eyes. My collarbones stuck out, my ribs were visible between my breasts. But my torso was proportioned just right, curved inward toward the waist and outward down the slope of the hip. It was and wasn't me I was looking at. I looked into my own eyes and laughed until I started to cry.

Suddenly I heard footsteps in the other room from the give of the old hardwood floor.

"Hi," Alix said. "You just get up?"

"I haven't slept," I said. "I took the rest of the acid. I'm sorry. But I feel so much better now."

"It's fine," she said. "Oh, I forgot to ask you before. You don't have a family history of schizophrenia, or borderline personality disorder, do you? Acid can really fuck you up if you've got a latent mental illness."

"I don't know," I said, "but I've always thought my mother was a classic case of borderline."

"Oh," she said. "Well, you're probably fine. You seem fine!"

I felt within me a destabilizing tension, a pulling apart, like I might actually fall to pieces.

I dressed, then went to the kitchen, where she was smoking a joint while ceremoniously preparing a pot of tea. My body advanced as if weightless. I entered her personal space with trepidation, closed the suspenseful question of distance between us. I put my hand on her shoulder, but felt nothing, touched nothing. She turned back toward me, head first, followed by the train of hair that fell over her shoulder-blades; her torso and hips swivelled around next, then her legs and bare feet followed; she pointed her toes to stick the landing. Her toes were long and slender, like mine. Her second toe was longer than her big toe, also like mine. She laid her sympathetic gaze upon me like a velvet-gloved hand, looked me in the eyes, and smiled.

"Your eyes are so fucking green right now!" she said.

"What?"

She handed me the joint.

"Usually your eyes are hazel, but right now, they're green. Bright green."

I took a drag as she took the tea set outside on a burnished brass tray: two hand-thrown clay cups in their saucer, and a glass pot steeping chamomile, peppermint, and rosehips. She'd laid a flower on the tray, I recognized it from one of the bushes in the front of the house. We sat cross-legged on a couple of cushions out on the porch with our tea. In the shade of the trees, the heat was just bearable. Birds sang out from the heights of the trees. A jacaranda was in bloom and raining acid-violet petals. I leaned into a sunbeam to feel the warmth on my face.

Her eyes shined at me, actually glittered, and I realized I was still tripping hard.

"What?"

"Hold on." She took her phone and, after searching for a minute, showed me a picture of a painting called 'Calla Lily Turned Away.'

"Tender, luminous white folds with soft, crooked edges, unfurling from this radiant dark-green stem… that's how you look when you're leaning earnestly into the light, like that."

I turned my head into the light at an angle, posing as the lily for her, smiling then breaking into laughter. She laughed, too, and we both said "I love you" at the same time, then laughed some more. Then we shared in a comfortable silence. I felt pure and alive, made of light.

"It's turning out to be a beautiful day," she said, and promptly dissolved into the ether.

Suddenly, as if swept under the waves by a riptide, I descended into a black ocean of consciousness. Every ambient sound took on a shape in the black behind my eyelids. Like a lava lamp. So I watched. I listened to myself breathe. One deep breath at a time, the racing thoughts slowed down a little more. I saw a flight of stairs in front of me, a grand old spiral staircase in dark light, and started walking down. I walked down ten flights of stairs, each level I descended dimmer than the last until I couldn't see where I was going, kept going by holding and sliding my hand down the railing. Advancing one step at a time. I saw myself as if watching ants in an ant farm, the earth around the tunnel of stairs made up of the dust of long buried, densely packed memories. I stepped off the last step onto the ground, felt and smelled earth. I felt around in the dark, no light and no sound, until I found a door, and I pushed it open.

I was in a dark room with just a candlestick lighting the center. I picked up the candle, then daylight blitzed my eyes and I was on a beach, standing before a little girl. She was sitting on her heels, digging in the wet sand, her toes dug into the mud as the waves lapped her feet. She was whole, unadulterated. Sparks zapped in the atmosphere around her like an invisible electrical grid short-circuiting. One wave came up strong and hit her from behind, dragged her body into the froth. My father as a young man ran past where I stood immobilized. He thrashed into the water and suddenly sank to his hips where the undertow had carved a ledge into the sand. I watched him reach into the churning water and pull up the toddler by her ankle. He held her up out of the water like a fisherman posing with a big catch. She sputtered and wailed as he carried her to shore.

With a hypnic jerk, I found myself back in my body, laying on the floor. I opened my eyes.

The ego is a prison, but a prison is only walls. In the aftermath of the acid flood in my brain was a panoramic vista of a lucid blue ocean.

So much time wasted on so much self-destruction, it seemed absurd to arrive at the conclusion that I wanted to live a good, long life. But I didn't want to live and die for my histrionics. I wanted to dominate and harness my internal chaos in service to my art.

I was named for a flower, *Zantedeschia aethiopica*. Consider nominative determinism. The calla lily is not a true lily. It is a very pretty fraud. It blooms in late spring. It is a popular choice for funerary decor. Let's agree nominative determinism is bunk. Then I should suggest a more fitting poetic stand-in for this particular I. Consider the ghost orchid. *Dendrophylax lindenii*. Its white blossom slouches from the weight of its tendrils, which resemble two legs spread out from its pelvis-petal. It is endangered in the wild but it resists captivity. Somehow it knows when it is not free and promptly gives up on living.

The only objective to telling a story is to finish it, to deliver the punchline. God am I tired of listening to myself talk.

For Barry and Sue

For their support throughout the creation of this book, the author thanks Alexandra M.F. Quicho, Ashley Opheim, Ales Kot, Jordan Robson-Cramer, Jaclyn Bruneau, Kylee Luce, and Szilvia Molnar.